MATED TO WOLVES

AMELIA SHAW

TAMSIN SHAW

CONTENTS

CHAPTER 1

JAYDY

Working at the magic school as the new potions master was challenging, to say the least, but I truly loved it. Teaching students coming through senior school and mentoring those who had fallen behind was the best part. As someone who'd never had magical capabilities that were considered very powerful, I loved being able to encourage others like me. There was a place for us in this world, and I'd made it my personal mission to help them not only find it but also embrace it.

The bell sounded, and I closed my books, packed up my classroom, and headed to the staff room to have some lunch. The other teachers at the school hadn't exactly warmed up to me just yet, but I wasn't giving up. I'd put up with bullies most of my life. A few less-than-friendly colleagues weren't going to get me down. I'd dealt with much worse during my formative years.

As I rounded the corner, I stopped mid-stride, hearing a sniggering female voice in the staff room.

"So that's how she got all her extra power... her fat ass! I *knew* she wasn't powerful enough to get a job here with us."

A few giggles later, another woman joined the conversation.

"Well, don't tell me I've got to turn into a fat cow to increase my magic, because quite frankly, I'd rather die."

Their laughter made me shudder, and their words made me bloody angry. The levels to which some people were willing to stoop to bring another down never ceased to appall me. With years of practiced courage and no small amount of resilience, I lifted my chin and walked into the room, going straight to the coffee machine as if I didn't have a care in the world. "Hey." I nodded at the two skinny women sitting at the table with their sad, unappetizing salad bowls in front of them.

"Hey," they responded robotically, their demeanors immediately changing. Lisa, the one on the left, turned red and looked like she'd been caught with her hand in the cookie jar.

At least she has the grace to feel ashamed of her behavior.

I grabbed my favorite pink and purple coffee mug and poured myself a cup. I was never one to go looking for confrontation but certainly wouldn't avoid it if it came looking for me. I was no coward, and regardless of their shallow opinions, loved the person I was and grown to become over the years.

Once my coffee was ready, after adding a healthy dollop of cream and two sugars, I headed to the table and sat down. "Are you talking about Tania or me?" I asked, lifting my eyebrows at them, waiting. I assumed they were talking about me, but big, powerful witches were more common now than they'd ever been. *Thanks to Harry.* I stared pointedly at the other two women sitting across the table from me.

Naomi, the bigger bitch of the two, grabbed her lunch and left without saying anything.

Lisa remained sitting there, looking at me like a deer in headlights.

"You don't need to lie," I told Lisa flatly. "I overheard what you two were talking about as I was walking in."

"It was Naomi, mostly," she whispered, then coughed to clear her throat. "But everyone's been talking about it."

"Talking about what?" I asked, taking a sip of my coffee before magicking up my lunch—a lamb wrap and a colorful fruit salad. I grabbed the wrap with two hands and took a bite, loving the burst of flavors assaulting my tongue. Marinated lamb, tomato and lettuce, with tzatziki.

"The spell," she said, shifting nervously in her chair. "The one that made you all better witches."

I tried not to laugh but couldn't smother the smile that rose to my lips. "You all? You mean… the big girls?"

Harry had granted Tania's wish, that us big girl witches would finally have magic that matched our strength and size. I hadn't noticed it at first, but it soon became apparent that the harder I trained at the gym, the more power I had at my disposal.

Lisa nodded. "Yeah. It was Harry, wasn't it? That cast the genie spell?"

I inhaled sharply, not sure how much I was allowed to reveal. The genie spell was forbidden in our community, but Harry's death had been high profile. Especially as his parents were on the council, and his death had been ruled a suicide. "I'm not sure how much I can say," I admitted. "But if you're interested in obtaining more magic, it's not just about size, it's about strength too. If you want to join us in training, Tania's gym is open to everyone."

Lisa stood up and gave me a half smile. "Thanks for the offer, but that's not really my style."

"Fair enough," I said and shrugged.

Lisa was a powerful witch anyway. It wasn't as if she needed more magic. She walked toward the door, then turned back to me unexpectedly. "I'm glad you're working here, Jaydy. Just so you know."

"Thanks," I said, appreciative for the kind words that I assumed were an attempt at an apology but kept my walls up. I couldn't trust anyone here. *Not yet.*

Lisa left me alone with my lunch.

I finished my kebab, drank a glass of water, and downed the fruit salad as well. I'd carb load later and already had a protein shake prepared for my post-gym workout.

The next two periods of teaching potions went quickly, and I was soon done for the day and on my way to Tania's gym—*Strong Geelong*. I pulled up at the front and secured my usual parking space. I smiled as I pulled in, looking forward to the energy of the workout ahead. I opened the car door and heard the characteristic thump of bass thrumming through the air.

The music coming from inside the gym was pumping hard, as usual, *Ramstein* if I wasn't wrong. Which could only mean one thing. "Yep, George is here already."

A smile lifted my lips as I grabbed my training duffel, a container of chicken from my cooler bag, as well as a protein shake, then headed inside. It was the night before Tania's wedding, so I didn't expect to see the bride-to-be, but her gym was open. *Of course.* Not even a "little thing" like a wedding was going to close Tania's gym.

Daniella was behind the reception desk, wearing her trademark grin.

I waved my hand in greeting. "Hey, Dani."

"Jaydy! How was your day?"

I shrugged as I swiped my membership card. "It was a day," I said simply. The cruel things that Lisa and Naomi had said were still sitting in the back of my mind, living rent free. I didn't want to admit to it, but what they'd said really bugged me. Learning to live with the insults didn't mean they hurt any less. "Hey, Dani," I said, deciding to ask her how she felt before losing the rest of the night to Naomi's vitriol, "How's your magic been since... you know."

Dani beamed at me, then lowered her voice conspiratorially. "You mean since the genie spell gave us all the power to match our booties?"

I laughed, unable to contain myself at her open and candid attitude. "Yeah, exactly."

Dani shrugged. "I haven't tried much, you know. I don't have a magical job, so I don't really need more magic, really. But I did—"

She glanced away, looking around as if she didn't want anyone to overhear our conversation.

"What?" I asked curiously, leaning forward so that she wouldn't have to speak as loud. "You did what?" I needed *something* interesting to occupy my mind.

She leaned over the counter and whispered with a sheepish grin, "I renovated my whole house!"

I couldn't help but laugh. "Really?"

She grinned at me as if shy and proud all at once. "I've been wanting to do it for years, but didn't have the money. But now..." she trailed off.

I clapped my hands and grinned at her, glad she'd been able to use her newfound levels of power to improve her life. "Good for you, girl. You deserve to enjoy it." The music in the gym shifted to a more upbeat, faster tempo, pulling me in. I waved to Dani, glancing over my shoulder as I headed to the squat rack. "See you later!" I called. "And I want see photos later."

"Anytime," Daniella said before returning to her duties at the desk.

"Jaydy!" George called out, waving from the corner where he was doing some deadlifts.

"Hey, George!" I greeted him, then got to work, lifting heavy. I was in training for the next Strong Woman competition in a few weeks. Tania wasn't much into competitions herself, but I loved them. The people, the atmosphere, the sense of achieving my personal goals. I'd even won a couple of times, but that wasn't the point—not for me—but now... I wasn't even sure I should be competing. After all, my new infusion of magic gave me a decidedly unfair advantage.

Not that I'd stopped training altogether, I couldn't. I loved it too much. It was my *me time*, and I liked taking care of my body as much as my mind. Loading up the bar, I put an extra five pounds on. It was more than I'd ever lifted before. Getting beneath the bar, I bent my knees, centered myself, and pressed up.

The weight was too much, and the breath was stolen from my lungs. Closing my eyes for a moment, I readied myself to call out to George and get him to take the weight off me, but it wasn't necessary. My magic rallied, shocking the hell out of me. Building a solid base in my gut, it moved out and down. I felt myself getting stronger, my muscles bulging as I stood up, before I went down into another squat. My thighs burned, my gut tightening as my core engaged.

Opening my eyes, I saw George standing, watching me intently, spotting me from afar.

"You all good?" he called out.

Sweat beaded on my brow but I managed a shaky smile. Pushing for one more squat, I put the bar back on the rack with a satisfied sigh. My legs shivered with pain, then power. The wave was like ecstasy, and I wanted more. I waved George over, my heart pumping. "Can you spot me? I'm going heavier."

The huge power lifter nodded. "Of course."

Then we got to work.

CHAPTER 2
JAYDY

The next day, I stood in Tania's parents' newly manicured backyard and watched my best friend walk down the aisle. She wore a stunning but simple, elegant white dress and held a bouquet of strikingly beautiful orange and purple flowers clutched in her hands. My eyes burned as tears swam, temporarily blurring my vision. I covered my mouth, suppressing my sniffles while trying not to sob out loud. Tania would laugh at me for being so emotional, so I tried not to let the tears of happiness swimming in my eyes fall and ruin my bridal party makeup.

I was so pleased for Tania, honestly unable to even articulate how happy I was. She was *such* a good woman, and she deserved to be treated well—more than well. She deserved the world. She should never have been left sitting on the shelf for so long, unloved and unappreciated. Those two wolf shifters who were now claiming her hands were the luckiest guys around. And yet, I knew it was Tania who felt like the lucky one. She'd told me as much.

I thought I'd managed to get my emotions under control, but my eyes welled with tears once more as I stared at the bride.

Tania's hand gripped her father's meaty arm, the pair completely taking up the wider than normal aisle. They were glorious, with huge smiles stretching from ear to ear.

The packed wedding ceremony was simple but sweet. I listened to every word, my heart thumping too fast in my chest. Tania's men really were so handsome, strong, and completely in love with her. Leo and Mason were awesome. They stood there, on either side of her, chests puffed and proud. My soul sang at the thought that they would—all three of them—take care of each other for the rest of their lives. It was breathtakingly romantic.

The reception afterward was being hosted at Tania's parents' home too. So, after the ceremony was finished, the bride and her grooms went to have their photographs taken. The rest of us were directed to a standing area for drinks and canapes while the chairs were magicked away, and the backyard was set up for the reception.

I wandered over to where they'd placed a bar and asked for a glass of white wine.

The bartender smiled and with a snap of his fingers, a glass appeared in front of me.

I could have done that myself technically, but it was nice having someone magically summon me a drink instead. "Thanks," I said with a smile to the warlock bartender before taking the drink and turning back to stare out over the reception area. The whole backyard had been decorated with matching flowers, a white marquee tent, and beautiful antique furniture. The area looked every bit as swanky as an expensive hotel, with the added bonus of being an intimate and special family gathering.

"Hello?" a male voice said from an area to my right.

I turned, not sure if the man was speaking to me, but not wanting to be rude if he was. There were two men standing there looking at me, not just one. They were both dressed in black suits for the wedding, as the dress code was formal, but I wasn't sure which one had spoken. Despite my best efforts to contain myself, my jaw dropped as I studied them.

They were staggeringly gorgeous. One light, the other dark, but both sexy as sin. And *they* were wearing their suits, not the other way around. And both were staring straight at me with an intensity that almost took my breath away. I swallowed hard and lifted my chin, dredging up my courage. There was no one else around, so they were definitely speaking to me. "Can I help you?" I asked.

The larger, blonder, more Viking-looking guy stumbled forward with his hand out. "I... *we* wanted to introduce ourselves. I'm Chase," he said.

I stared at his hand for a moment and decided I should be polite and introduce myself too. "I'm Jaydy." I reached out and shook his hand, a frisson of electricity passing through me at the touch of his skin against mine. I gasped audibly and quickly pulled my arm back, curling my fingers into my palm in shock.

What the hell was that?

The Viking rubbed his hand against his thigh, shivering in an obvious way from head to toe.

The air between us was suddenly buzzing with electricity I hadn't expected, so I tried awkwardly for a joke to help break the tension. "I'd assumed you were from the wolf shifter side of the family... but with a zap like that, are you sure you aren't a warlock?"

The guys glanced at each other and shared a strange look I couldn't interpret.

I pulled my gaze away from them with a concerted effort. My stomach lurched and my throat thickened with emotion. I wasn't sure what was wrong with me, but suddenly, I was having trouble breathing and felt the urgent need to run. I began to back away as calmly as I could manage. "Ah, there's a few of Tania's cousins I've been meaning to catch up with. So, if you'll excuse me, I might just... go." I moved to take another step away but stopped when the darker-haired guy spoke.

"We *are* wolf shifters, you're right," said. "We're brothers and pack mates of Mason and Leo. We grew up with them."

The way they were looking at me was making me uncomfortable. Men like them didn't normally bother speaking to the someone like me. I was a not skinny, single, over thirty-year-old witch, and without a particularly huge amount of power.

Well, that isn't so true anymore.

Thanks to the sudden increase in my powers from the genie's granted wish, I'd landed a new job, and my life was kind of turning around for the better. But not enough that two men who looked like *that* would ever waste time talking to me.

Unless...

I stopped trying to creep away and consciously tried to relax and put on my professional face. "Is this about a spell?" I prompted. That was likely the reason they'd come to me.

Maybe they need help, as Mason and Leo had?

"Tania's more powerful than me," I admitted, "but if you need my help with something, I'm happy to listen and see what I can do."

"Yes!" The Viking said, a little too forcefully. "Yes... *exactly*. That's why we're here. That's what we need."

"Sorry about my brother," the other, darker guy added, his casual confidence as hot as an inferno. "We know this is a wedding and everything, but could we perhaps grab your number?"

"To ask for my help with a spell?" I asked again, wanting to get it straight in my head as to exactly what they wanted, given the strangeness of this whole interaction. The dark-haired guy's smile in response was one for the record books, and I had to lock my knees so as to not collapse.

"Yeah... Or..."

"Or, what?" I asked, suspicion rising within me, making me anxious. I crossed my arms over my chest defensively, closing off my welcoming body language and staring at them hard. When both of their gazes dropped in identical perfect timing to my breasts, I dropped my arms away just as fast.

Damn it.

My face flushed with heat. I was wearing a beautiful, formal dress for the occasion, but I'd forgotten how low-cut it was, and just how well-endowed I was.

"Or a date maybe?" the Viking asked, coughing to clear his throat. "Or two?"

The brothers grinned at me.

I took a tentative step back and pursed my lips before answering. "Look... guys, I'm flattered, but trust me, I'm not your type. I'm pretty boring, among other things."

The men followed my lead, moving forward as I walked backward. It was like they were kind of stalking me, as if their wolves were on the prowl and I was in their sights.

"We doubt that very much," the dark-haired one said, and I realized I still didn't know his name.

I began to panic. They were advancing, their eye contact unbroken. They were serious, and I felt well out of my depth. "Oh, no. You see... ah."

"Jaydy!"

I turned to the sound of a familiar male voice booming my name. "Jack!" I cried with relief, hugging Tania's huge father when he came up to me. "It's so nice to see you."

Jack turned to the wolf shifters. "Thanks for keeping Jaydy company, boys."

They nodded at me and spoke in unison. "It was nice to meet you." Then they very slowly walked away and strangely, they seemed disappointed.

"You okay, Jaydy?" Jack asked, poking me with his elbow. "You looked like you wanted some help, not that you really needed it. Your magic could blast those two away in an instant." Jack shook his head at the shifters as they walked away. As a lifelong warlock, Jack had a natural dislike of the shifting side of the paranormal.

I tried not to laugh at him. He now had two wolf shifter sons-in-law, so he really needed to ease up on his prejudices. I grinned up at the giant of a man and changed the subject, just glad I could finally breathe again. "It's nice to see Tania happy, isn't it?"

Jack grunted in acknowledgement. "Yeah, even if it is with two wolf shifters."

I laughed at his tone. "You *love* Mason and Leo. I've seen how you are with them."

He shrugged. "Yeah, well luckily those two are different."

My gaze tugged away from Jack and back toward the two wolf shifters who were still lingering nearby. "Yeah... I suppose there's always an exception to the rule," I answered vaguely, feeling oddly distracted.

Jack slung an easy arm around me. "Let's go find my wife," he suggested. "She'll be torturing the chef, I'm sure."

I let Jack pull me away from the men and kept myself busy all night. I'd had my heart broken before, and I wasn't about to offer it up on a silver platter to be smashed again. I couldn't bear that level of agony. Not twice. Once was more than enough for several lifetimes, as far as I was concerned.

CHAPTER 3

DAMON

G oing home alone after the wedding was one of the hardest things I'd ever done. That curvy, gorgeous, blonde witch was our mate, and we should have been balls deep in her perfect body by now. If she'd been a shifter too, we would have been. She would have known who we were to her from the moment our gazes first met.

Instead, it was after midnight, and we were sitting in our newly renovated kitchen together. Just Chase and I, as always. I felt so angry, I could barely think straight. It was as if a dark storm cloud was roiling in my mind, and I couldn't shake it. Its shadow lingered over me and within me, frustrating the hell out me.

"Hey," Chase called out to me as he wandered into the kitchen. "Do you want a beer?"

I shook my head, then realized he couldn't see it from where he was. "No. I want to run." We'd already consumed our weight in beer tonight. It had been the only thing that had kept me seated and remotely sane while I'd been forced to watch my mate dancing away with her friends on the dance floor.

Damn, she was hot.

I'd gotten up several times, a growl catching in my throat as I fought to keep control over my shifter. I wanted her so desperately, I could almost crawl out of my own skin.

Chase stepped back into the living room, a single beer in hand for himself.

I tore off the restrictive jacket I was still wearing and pulled at my tie. "Do you want to come?"

Chase frowned at me. "You're still upset about Jaydy?"

I glared at my brother. "Of course, I am! Are you mad? We should have wooed her, brought her home."

"She didn't like us," Chase stated flatly. "We're going to have to take things slowly with her and get her used to the idea. And besides... I didn't ask you, but do you even care that she's *my* mate too?"

I shrugged, pushing aside that part of the equation that I'd steamrolled over at the wedding.

"What does that mean?" Chase pushed, squaring his shoulders with an annoyed look on his face.

I made the same gesture again as my irritation continued to skyrocket. "It means I don't know. I don't care about that. All I want is *my* mate."

"*Our* mate," Chase corrected adamantly, driving home the point he was trying to make.

I growled loudly and tore off my shirt, my wolf rising inside me hard and fast after being kept down for so long. "Yes! *Our* mate!" I practically yelled at him. "I don't care about all that shit! Leo and Mason share Tania, so why the hell wouldn't we Jaydy?"

Chase stared at me.

Then it occurred to me that my little brother might be the one with the problem. "Are you serious?" I demanded. "You don't want to share a mate with me?"

His eyes widened slightly, then he began to laugh.

I was about to lose it. Tonight had been one of the most frustrating nights of my life and my fucking brother was laughing at me.

I tore off my stupid suit pants and marched toward the back door. "I'm going."

Chase grabbed my arm as I tried to storm past him. "Go," he encouraged. "Get all this whatever it is out of your system. But I have no issue with sharing a mate with you. Got it?"

I managed to nod, then ran out the rear door. Our house backed onto the edge of the forest, like most of the shifter's homes in town. The back fence was low, and as I began running for the boundary, my wolf took over with wild abandon. Fur sprouted through my skin, and my body transformed into my wolf between one breath and the next. Now on all fours, I ran for the fence and jumped. I soared over the pickets, but not stopping there, I ran and ran until my lungs burned and my paws ached.

I'd thought about my mate for years now. Ever since turning thirty, which was three years ago. I'd wanted a Fated mate, but hadn't known if that would happen for me. I'd dated shifters from our pack and humans from town. Anyone my wolf suspected might be a possible match. However, they'd all led to disappointment and once or twice, a little heartbreak. But the moment I'd seen Jaydy, I'd known. Balls to bones... I'd known. She was mine.

When Chase had shaken hands with her, she'd felt it too. I'd seen it in her face—the surprise and the shock. She'd even commented on the feeling. The frisson. The zap of attraction. The acknowledgement of what we were to each other.

And yet, she'd rejected me... well, *us*. She'd gone back to the party and danced the night away without any admission of what she'd just experienced, or how much we needed her.

Was this how Mason and Leo had started their relationship with Tania? With rejection and blue balls? It was hard to believe that, given they were so madly in love now.

I jumped a log and darted around a tree, running until I at last reached the river. There, I drank from its flowing waters, and when my ridiculous heart continued to race like it was participating in a marathon, I jumped into the cold water and swam for a while, soaking away and chilling the heat from my head, heart, and bones.

When I was finally settled enough, I turned around and made the slow trek back home. I had so many questions that needed answers. How were we going to convince Jaydy to give us a chance? Especially when her first response had been abject horror. She seemed to think the only reason we'd wanted to talk to her was for her magical abilities. Was she blind? She was fucking gorgeous! She was perfect for us. There was so much of her to love. I wanted to kiss every inch of every curve of her beautiful body. I was certain that once she agreed to start dating us, she'd fall head over heels.

Fate will take care of that. It has to.

And how did I *really* feel about sharing a mate with my brother? I searched my subconscious by mentally looking under all the rocks where men tended to hide their feelings, but all I found was a deep relief that I'd finally found her. That *we'd* found her. She was within reach. We knew who she was...

Chase and I were close and always had been. We owned a home together and even worked together. He was a good guy, and a much calmer, more relaxed man than I was. In many ways, it seemed like a great idea to share the workload of being a husband to a woman like her. She was obviously beautiful, big, and powerful, but she was also a witch.

Maybe having two of us will mean she'll never wander or feel unfulfilled?

I could only hope. I didn't know what Fate's plan was for us was, but it was abundantly obvious she had a sense of humor. We were the second set of brothers to fall for a single witch. How many more pairings could there be within our pack? Not that it mattered right now. Other wolves' romances weren't my problem. All I knew was that I wanted Jaydy, and I wanted her *now*. But I didn't even know where she lived, so that made the night's impromptu quest impossible.

I made my way back to our huge house, jumped the fence once

more, and shifted back to my human form. My skin chilled immediately in the cool night air, so I walked inside through the laundry entrance and locked the door behind me. From the silence that filled the air, I had to assume my brother was already asleep, so I had a quick, hot shower and went to bed myself.

Jaydy's vibrant smile haunted my dreams, and I woke in the morning light to a pounding headache and a stiff, aching cock. Despite the pain, I was strung out as fuck, so I dealt with myself, then crawled out of bed looking for some ibuprofen. Chase was already in the kitchen, cooking up breakfast.

"Morning," he offered.

The smell of the frying bacon turned my stomach, so I grabbed a cold bottle of water from the fridge and the pain killers from the cupboard. "Morning," I muttered back, feeling sorry for myself.

Chase continued with breakfast, seemingly calm and at peace, completely unlike me.

I found a seat on one of the kitchen stools and downed my bottle of water. The cold hit my belly hard, but I swallowed it down, needing the hydration after all the beer yesterday. My whole body felt like shit, and I hated it.

"I've got a plan," Chase said suddenly, serving up the eggs and bacon and placing a plate in front of me. He'd made toast, baked beans, and tomatoes too.

I swallowed hard and picked up a fork. "Thanks." I needed the energy and the calories as a shifter, but the smell was still making me feel ill. The first bite of greasy bacon was both heaven and hell. My stomach rebuked my efforts to balance the alcohol from last night, but at the same time, I managed to not toss my cookies. I didn't stop. I just kept forcing more food down my throat like I was pouring gas into the car.

Chase stood over me with an expectant look on his face.

"What?" I finally asked, my mouth half full of eggs.

"I said I have a plan," he repeated, crossing his arms over his chest, "to get Jaydy."

I sat up straighter and lifted my head, my shifter rising up inside me to give me a temporary wave of strength. That was a plan I wanted to hear. "Tell me."

"We go to her and ask her to do a spell for us, just like Mason and Leo did with Tania. It worked for them and will give us the time and space to get to know Jaydy, and her to know us. It's a win-win."

I frowned at him, my brows furrowing. "What sort of spell are you thinking?" It wasn't like we needed money or a house or anything.

His face sobered, then he finally spoke. "Tabitha," he said simply.

I actually dropped the fork I was holding. It clattered onto the plate before falling to the marble counter. "Do you seriously think she's powerful enough to help Tabby?" I'd thought about asking Tania to help us with Tabby when we'd first learned there was a witch willing to help us shifters, but I'd dismissed the thought just as quickly. Tabby's injuries were old and severe. If her shifter genes weren't strong enough to heal her, what hope did magic have?

Chase shrugged, leaning on the counter as he grabbed a piece of crispy bacon between his fingers and crunched down on it. "I don't know, but she said last night that she'd try if we had something we needed help with."

Tania was on her honeymoon with Mason and Leo at the moment, so at least Jaydy wouldn't be able to try and push us onto her friend if we did ask. "Okay," I said, nodding my head and shoveling more food into my mouth. "When should we go?" It was a Sunday morning, so we didn't have to work.

"Today?" Chase suggested, raising a hopeful eyebrow.

I laughed, hope, and happiness bubbling up inside of me of me in turn. "I like the way you think."

Chase grinned and grabbed his own breakfast, devouring it at breakneck speed.

I took another sip of water, then a thought occurred to me, and my chest was suddenly tight. "Do you think we should talk to Tabby or Mom and Dad first? You know, before speaking to Jaydy about her..."

Our baby sister had been badly injured as a child. She'd survived, mostly thanks to her rapid healing and shifter genes, but she was permanently paralyzed from the waist down. It was a tragedy and something we wished we could fix with all our big brotherly hearts.

Chase inhaled swiftly, then sighed. "I've thought about that too, but I think we should talk to Jaydy first. There's no point in getting Tabby's hopes up if magic can't do anything to help her. It's best we figure out what the chances are before we say anything."

"True," I agreed. Tabby was a beautiful girl, who had a kind soul and a sassy attitude to match. She didn't deserve the fate she'd been dealt. It was a cruel hand. I cleaned up my plate and washed the dishes before retreating to my room to get ready for the gym. I had no idea if Jaydy would turn up the day after a wedding, or when, but since we'd failed to get her cell number last night, finding her at Tania's gym was the best bet we had.

"Let's go," I called out to my brother, eager to secure our mate and hopefully help our sister.

Chase jogged into the lounge room in a pair of sweats and a tank. "Yep. Let's do it."

We headed out the door and hopped in the truck.

"Do we know anyone we could ask for help with this?" Chase asked.

I started the truck and headed toward Tania's gym. We didn't have a lot of contacts in the magical world, so our options were limited. "George, maybe?" I suggested. He was a warlock who'd been friends with the shifters in our pack for years.

Chase got out his cell phone. "I'll text him now."

We drove through the suburbs and toward the industrial side of the city where Tania's gym resided. For the first time since Jaydy had walked away from us, I smiled. We had a direction, and hope had rekindled inside my heart.

This could really work.

CHAPTER 4
CHASE

We arrived at the gym just as George answered our texts. I stared down at the screen on my cell phone and read it aloud. "George says Jaydy usually trains late afternoon, but with the wedding yesterday, it's anyone's guess what her schedule will be."

Damon parked the truck, and we got out. The smile on my brother's face was one I'd never seen. He looked excited, almost ready to burst, but strangely nervous as well.

Is he feeling the same gut-wrenching sense of anticipation I am?

Damon grabbed our duffel out of the backseat. It was packed with water bottles, body spray, and spare shirts for our normal day-to-day lives. "I'm up for a full day at the gym," he said brightly, clearly determined to remain until we saw Jaydy again.

I chuckled. "Yeah, I thought you might say that. It's only ten am. You realize we might be hanging around for another eight hours?"

Damon shrugged. "We stay as long as it takes."

With a shared nod, we headed inside.

The first person I saw when we entered was a woman behind the desk. She was obviously a power lifter too, judging by her wide shoulders and even bigger smile.

"Hi, guys," she greeted us. "Are you here to join?" Her nametag said *Daniella*, but I couldn't recall seeing her at the wedding.

Damon walked straight up to the desk with an enviable amount of confidence. "Yeah, hi, we are. Tania's a family friend of ours."

Daniella grinned. "You must be related to Mason and Leo then."

I moved beside my brother, joining him at the counter. "We are," I confirmed. "I'm Chase and this is Damon."

"Brothers?" she asked with a raised eyebrow.

I couldn't help but laugh. "Yeah, how'd you guess?" We looked nothing alike. I had our mother's lighter coloring, blue eyes, and short blond hair, whereas Damon was darker, just like our father.

She shrugged like it was no big deal, but there was a mysterious, knowing twinkle in her eye.

I grinned at her, instantly clueing in. "You're a witch too."

She put her finger to her lips. "Shhh..." she warned. "We have humans here." But then she winked playfully at me to soften the effect. "I'll get you guys some forms." She returned a second later, handing us each a clipboard.

We filled in our details quickly, opting to tick the yearly option. We may as well have a gym membership to catch up with Tania and my cousins when we could, and it's not like we couldn't afford the expense.

"Would you like a tour now?" Daniella asked.

But before I could respond, Daniella called out over the divide between the reception desk and the gym, "Hey, Jaydy! Are you up for a quick tour?"

"Sure, no problem!" she called back.

Damon grabbed my arm, his face lighting up like he was a kid on Christmas morning.

I glanced at him briefly before shaking my head at him. I wanted to yell, "I know! Be cool!" But it was obvious Damon was about to burst out of his clothes on the spot, which said a lot about just how much our Fated mate affected us. He was usually the suave and stoic one of few words.

Jaydy came around the corner with a big smile on her face... which dropped from her lips the moment she laid eyes on us. "What are you two doing here?" she asked, her brow furrowing ever so slightly.

I tried to stay cool. "Mason and Leo suggested we join the gym, and since we had the day free..."

Daniella handed Jaydy the two clipboards with our details. "Are they friends of yours?"

Jaydy swallowed hard, as if she were finding it difficult to speak. "We met at the wedding last night."

Daniella grinned. "Oh, lovely. So, everyone is acquainted. Well, boys... enjoy!" She waved us off and turned to help the people walking in the door behind us.

Jaydy stared down at the clipboards. "Okay... well, let's get started. Damon and Chase, follow me." She turned on her heel.

As Jaydy walked off, my gaze dropped to her backside, and I had to resist the urge to growl. The stretchy black material of her leggings hugged her voluptuous ass in a way that made my mouth water.

Damn, she is fine.

Damon was frozen in place, like someone had hit pause on a remote, leaving him stranded between one breath and the next.

I walked forward, giving my brother a nudge on the way past. "Let's go."

"We're predominantly a powerlifting gym," she explained, gesturing to the numerous posters and shining award plaques on the wall. "You don't have to compete, of course, but most of our bars, weights, and specialized equipment have been designed for lifting big."

We followed her over to a corner in the room set up with racks holding traditional dumbbells.

"We have personal trainers here who can set you up with a

program to help get you started in the right direction if you're interested."

Jaydy was so close now, I couldn't refrain from inhaling deeply and filling my nose with her amazing scent. She was wearing something a little floral, and her sweat smelled sweet.

She whirled to glare at me for invading her personal space, almost smacking me with her blonde ponytail in the process.

"Do you do that?" I managed to ask, saving myself from embarrassment.

She stopped, refusing to answer for several breathless moments that felt like a literal eternity before she finally nodded.

"Oh, great," I said with a grin. "Is there any chance that you can you help us out today?"

"I'm actually heading home soon," she said, lifting her chin in that funny move she seemed to make when she was trying to raise a wall between us.

"Maybe next time," Damon said stiffly, though I could feel his palpable disappointment.

But I wasn't going to let this opportunity pass by, so I pivoted and reached out to grab her arm as she turned away. "Hey, sorry, but are you still able to help us with a spell?"

She turned back to me, her expression softer and more open with concern. "I don't know," she admitted. "You'll have to tell me a little about what you need."

I glanced around, aware of humans not too far away using the gym too. "Is there somewhere we can chat?" I suggested hopefully, keeping my tone even and approachable.

Jaydy nodded, her kind heart evident. She might be able to blow us off with a clear conscience when it came to a workout, but when it came to magic, she clearly took matters far more seriously. She wouldn't turn away someone in need. "Yeah, sure. Let's use Tania's office. She isn't here today."

"Oh, yeah. She's on her honeymoon, right?" Damon said, following close behind her.

"They've gone to Hawaii for a month."

I laughed out loud. "Really? Wow. They'll be the talk of the hotel for sure."

Jaydy actually snorted as she half-laughed, her cheeks flushing with momentary color. "Oh my God, I hadn't thought about that!"

I grinned at her. "Two brothers fawning over their one gorgeous woman? Sounds like a dream to me."

Her smile disappeared as she opened the door to Tania's office. She'd obviously understood my none-too-subtle double meaning and didn't appreciate the suggestion. "Come on in," she said, avoiding meeting my gaze.

The office was small but served its purpose. There was a large desk with piles of paperwork and a small computer for administration and accounting work.

"Where do the stairs lead?" I asked, pointing to a spiral staircase in the corner of the room.

Damon took a seat, back to his normal darkly observant self.

I sat down beside him, giving Jaydy no choice but to sit in the chair behind Tania's desk.

"Tania's apartment," she answered, then sat and pulled herself into the desk, clasping her hands together as if to say, *let's get down to business.* "All right, tell me how I can help you."

I grinned at her, happy to be able to speak properly. "Well, I know I didn't get to introduce myself officially yesterday, but I'm Chase, and this is my brother, Damon."

She nodded at me, glancing at Damon for a moment before giving me her attention again. Her eyes were so clear and blue, they were like lakes sparkling beneath the summer sun.

Damon nudged me with his knee, drawing me from my thoughts.

Clearing my throat, I realized I'd stopped talking and was instead staring at Jaydy intently.

"Oh, sorry... the spell, right. We're not even sure if it's possible," I admitted.

Damon leaned forward in his chair, ready to pick up the slack where I'd dropped the ball, quite literally lost in her eyes like some kind of lovesick pup. "I asked Mom about it a while ago, when Tania helped Mason and Leo's parents return."

Tania sat up straighter. "So you're serious about me helping you with a spell? This isn't just some elaborate way of asking me out again?"

I almost swallowed my tongue at her frankness and ended up coughing to hide my reaction. "Well..."

Fuck.

"We definitely need your help," Damon said, carefully not addressing the dating part.

"It's a family issue?" Jaydy asked, the compassion in her gaze growing.

I sobered. This was serious, and I needed to calm my wolf and focus on our sister. There would be time for us later, I was sure. "Yeah, our baby sister, Tabby."

"Well, Tabitha's not a baby anymore," Damon clarified with a subtle smile. "She's twenty-one."

Jaydy smiled gently in return, the prettiest look passing over her face as if overcome by pleasant, heart-warming memories of the past. "I know what you mean. I have a younger brother, and even though he's six feet tall and twenty now, I still think of him as my baby brother. I probably always will."

I swallowed hard, struggling to focus again. Everything about her, despite her earlier efforts to shield herself and freeze us out, spoke of tenderness and inner beauty.

Stay focused.

Jaydy shifted in her chair and jumped straight back to business. "So, how can I help her?" she prompted. "The more information I've got, the better."

I exhaled slowly, recalling the details with a pained grimace. "When Tabby was young, she was hit by a car."

Jaydy inhaled sharply, her eyebrows shooting up and her breath catching in her throat. "Is she okay?"

"Well, she survived the incident," I said "thanks to her shifter genetics. But her back was broken in the accident, and that has never improved. She's in a wheelchair."

"And the doctors say she'll be paralyzed for the rest of her life," Damon added as if to drive home the seriousness of the matter.

Jaydy stood up and began pacing the room, visibly agitated. "I don't know if I can help you with her. I mean, I'd love to, of course. That poor girl. But I'm not a master of healing magic, not by any stretch of imagination."

I desperately wanted to reach out and touch her. My wolf was practically howling inside my head to claim my mate, but she was sending out all sorts of *professional* vibes right now. "Hey, if you don't mind my asking... what do you do for work?"

She turned and stared at me, hesitating a moment before answering. "Ah... I'm a potions professor at the magic high school. I find teaching quite rewarding."

"That's kind of cool," Damon said, giving me a look.

I slid to the edge of the chair. If magic was her job, then surely, she could do something to help? "Does that mean you might be able to conjure up a potion for Tabby?"

Jaydy frowned, tilted her head, then began pacing again. "I don't know. I mean, I am more powerful now than I ever have been because of the genie spell, but that doesn't mean I can necessarily undo spinal cord damage. That's a really serious injury."

I glanced over at Damon and raised my eyebrows curiously. "Genie spell?"

Jaydy sighed and waved her hand dismissively. "Don't worry about it."

"So, will you try?" I asked as gently as I could. "Or at least ask around for us? See if someone knows anything that might help? Please? We've never investigated this before, so we don't really know what's even possible."

Jaydy walked forward, pressing her knuckles to the desk as she leaned forward and stared at us. "How come? I mean... why did you never investigate what magic could do for your sister years ago?"

Damon gave her a lopsided smile. "We were only sixteen or so when it happened, and the witches didn't exactly like us wolf shifters back then. Our history hasn't been... friendly."

Jaydy stared at Damon long and hard as if weighing her options. "Well, things have changed since then. I'll definitely look into it for you."

I reached for my wallet and handed her one of my business cards.

She stared at it for a full minute in silence. "You're an attorney?"

"One for shifters mostly, yeah," I said, grabbing our bag. "Damon is one too, so if you call that line and can't get me, just ask for him."

Damon grabbed a pen from the desk, thinking fast. "I'll write my cell number on the back if you like?"

Jaydy mutely handed back the card and Damon did exactly that. My number was on the front anyway, so at least she had everyone's details now. "Okay, well, I'll speak to you both soon then."

She was dismissing us, that much was clear, which I found rather amusing. Most people in our community showed us a lot of respect, which often translated into submissive behavior. But this was different.

She's different. She's strong.

"Of course," I said, thanking her as I opened the door, and we waved our goodbyes.

Damon followed me to the bench press.

I set down our bag and began to add weights to the bar.

"You still want to train for a bit?" he asked hopefully.

"Fuck, yeah," I said as I rolled down onto my back. Adrenaline was coursing through me like a river, and while I couldn't shift, I could exercise. "That was a great first step, but my wolf is frustrated as shit."

Damon groaned in understanding. "Mine too. She smells fucking divine." He sighed.

I gritted my teeth as I adjusted my grip on the bar. "Go train," I urged, needing to be alone for a minute.

Damon chuckled as he walked away. He understood better than anyone what I was feeling and going through right now because he was in the exact same damn boat.

With determination, I threw myself into my workout session. Jaydy had left the building already, and I could feel the lack of her warmth in the very air around us. But what hadn't left me was the incredible desire to be near her... and the frustration of being pushed away.

She'll warm up to us. She's got to. Fate is never wrong...

CHAPTER 5
JAYDY

The wolf shifters' plight had tugged at my heartstrings like nothing else had before. I couldn't even *imagine* something like that happening to my beloved younger brother, Benny. I would have moved heaven and earth to get his legs back, and now that I knew about Tabby, I'd attempt the same for her. If there was anything at all I could do to improve her quality of life, I would.

My first stop post gym was my home library, where I searched out healing spells, bone broths, and potions for skeletal re-growth. But everything I found was for a new fracture, or something that wasn't nearly as serious as Tabby's long-term injury. "If only they'd asked for help ten years ago." I shook my head in dismay as I sat down on my barrel chair, tucking my legs under me so I could continue my research.

I still had many books to go study, but I was almost certain I didn't have what I needed. The school library was infinitely larger than anything I had, and the school principal himself was a renowned healer, or had been many years ago.

Perhaps he'd help me if I asked?

I picked up my cell phone and searched for the business card

Chase had given me. My hands shook as I held the card up, even though I reminded myself to be cool. There was something special about those two men, but their interest in me was worrying. I'd managed to hold the line so far, but how long would I remain steadfast if they actively pursued me and went on the charm offensive?

I made a loud snorting noise, forgetting myself. "As if they're going to ask me out again." I allowed myself to shake my head and laugh. "Girl, you're getting *way* ahead of yourself."

A moment later, my black cat jumped up on the couch and padded over to stand on my knee. "Hello, Meg, my beautiful girl." I kissed her head, and she purred loudly in response to my affection. "Did you think I was talking to you, sweetheart? Sorry, no. Mommy was just talking to herself." Which was something I did far too often, living alone.

I grabbed my cell phone and typed in both the guys' numbers, not wanting to leave either out. My heart pounded faster than it should have, considering this was *just* a job. "No need to get excited over messaging two guys who just want me for my magic," I told myself. Taking a deep breath, I typed a simple text.

Hey, guys, it's Jaydy. Just letting you know that none of my magic books at home have the spells or information I need, so I'll do a deep dive at the magic school tomorrow and touch base with other professors as well.

Within mere seconds I got two messages back in quick succession.

Thanks so much. You're perfect.

From Chase.

Thanks for keeping us in the loop. Can't wait for tomorrow's update.

From Damon.

I stared down at my phone and struggled not to immediately message them back. The very idea that they might be serious about dating me was horrifying. The last serious relationship I'd had lasted five years. He'd been a warlock and someone who'd known me well. But when people had started hinting that we should be getting engaged by my thirtieth birthday, he'd moved out so fast he'd left a dust cloud in his wake.

He was living with some twenty-year-old witch on the other side of the city now. "And we don't miss him at all, do we, Meggy?" I lifted the cat up and she yowled deep in her throat, knowing exactly who I was talking about. I laughed. "Yeah, I know, honey. You never liked him."

And she hadn't. I'd soon learned that my gorgeous kitty was the best judge of character, even when I wasn't. I snorted out a laugh, a horrible habit of mine that I sincerely hated, then sighed. "I wonder what you'd think about the two wolf shifters I'm working with, huh? Cats and dogs are natural enemies, right?" Meg didn't respond and instead returned to curling up on my lap.

I ran my fingers through her fur, closed my eyes, and settled on the couch. There was a big week ahead of me with school exams coming up and it was definitely the right choice to turn in and have an early night. Regrettably, I moved from the comfort of the couch and went to bed. Before long, I fell asleep in the middle of my huge bed, with Meg curled up snuggly under my chin. If I ever worried about being lonely forever, the heat of her small, furry body against my chest always reassured me that I wasn't in fact alone. And that was enough.

THE NEXT DAY I had several periods off to prepare for my students' exams, but I was well ahead of schedule. So, I took that time to visit the library and make ground on my research. I couldn't stop thinking about Tabby and her injury. How horrible was the accident for her wolf shifter genes to not be able to heal her? I'd never heard of such a thing before.

What am I up against?

I didn't know a lot about shifters, having grown up with magical parents as well as going to the magic school. Neither my parents nor the school were particularly fond of shifters. So, on a whim, I grabbed a book on wolf shifters out of the library as well.

Better to be over-prepared than under.

When the school bell finally rang to signal the day was once again done, instead of heading straight to my car, I went to the principal's office instead. The door was shut, but I knocked and waited.

"Come in."

I pushed open the door and walked inside, closing it behind me for the sake of discretion. The principal, Professor Olden, was a man well into his sixties, and had once been a *very* powerful warlock.

"Professor Turnball," he greeted me. "What can I do for you?"

Summoning whatever grit I had, I dove down the proverbial rabbit hole. "May I have a moment of your time?" I asked. "I have a question about healing magic and was hoping you could suggest a direction to take."

The principal indicated to the chairs in front of his large desk. "Of course, I'm all ears. Please, take a seat."

I did as he directed, then got straight into the issue. "I've been asked to help a family friend..."

Well, sort of.

"And I don't know where to start. I can't find anything in any of the books I've scoured, so I'm at a bit of a loss."

"And what's their health concern?" Professor Olden asked.

I inhaled sharply, knowing before answering that he was going to be shocked to hear of the severity of Tabby's injuries. "Well, Tabitha is twenty-one years old, and she was in a car accident when she was a child. The impact caused a spinal injury. She's been in a wheelchair ever since."

Professor Olden's bushy eyebrows bounced up, and he steepled his fingers in thought. "So, she's paralyzed? And has been for what? Ten years?"

I nodded, leaving out the part about her being a wolf shifter, even though I knew it was important. Professor Olden, like most warlocks, didn't like anyone outside our magical circles—not even humans.

"I don't think anything can be done, especially if magic has been tried before," he said slowly, his lips pressing into a thin line. "That's a *very* old injury, and a severe one."

My shoulders slumped. "Damn it... I thought if anyone knew of a spell or a potion that might be able to help, it would be you. They're not magical, so they've never utilized healing magic to help the injury."

The professor frowned but didn't ask what Tabitha was, instead flexing his fingers in front of himself, nodding slowly. "There is one thing..." he said, trailing off, his eyes narrowing in thought.

"Tell me, please," I requested without hesitation, sliding right to the edge of my chair.

He got up slowly, walking over to the large bookcase on the opposite wall, then pulled a huge leather-bound book from the shelf. Dust puffed off the ancient-looking and very thick tome in a faint cloud as he drew it toward himself.

"Is that a healing book?" I asked, my entire focus captured.

"Not exactly," he said, bringing the book over, then laying it on the desk in front of me. "It's an old book, one of my grandfather's, actually. It has some very complicated spells, most of which I'd never attempt myself. But I've been told that you have recently come into significantly more power, Professor Turnball, so it may be possible that you will find what you need in here." He leaned forward and tapped the embossed leather for emphasis before leaning back in his chair.

I ignored the comment about my extra power and reached out for the book. Thanks to Tania and her parents, everyone knew about the genie spell Harry had cast and the effect it had on us big, powerful girls. It hadn't been my wish and wasn't my choice, but I wasn't going to look a gift horse in the mouth. My new magic was awesome, and the harder I trained, the greater it would be. It seemed like a fair trade-off to me, and I loved it.

"Thank you," I said, feeling a strange shiver wash over me as I clutched the book with both hands. I could feel the power in its pages, the whispers of long-forgotten spells stirring.

"I will warn you that the spells within are complicated, and the potions..." He whistled. "It's likely you won't even be able to find half the ingredients any longer. But if there's any chance of helping your friend, I believe you'll find it in there."

I stood up, holding the spell book to my chest like the prized possession and family heirloom it was. "Thank you so much, Professor Olden. I really appreciate this." I moved back toward the office door and pushed it open.

"You know, I wasn't sure about hiring you when you first applied. I don't mind being honest about that," he called out as I was leaving.

I turned back to smile at him. "I know." He'd made his dislike of me at the interview quite apparent.

"But I'll also be the first to admit when I'm wrong," the old teacher said, coughing loudly to clear his throat. "You're doing well here, and the students like you. You seem to be having a positive effect on their learning."

I managed to keep my smile in place despite the subtle under-handed nature of the compliment. "I'm enjoying being here and sharing my love of potion making." I held out the book in front of me, ending the conversation. "Thank you for this, again. I'll bring it back when I can."

"No rush, Professor." He waved his hand at me, dismissing me.. "I haven't used it in years." And he didn't seem to have any plans to.

With a chest full to bursting with hope and nervous energy, I left quickly, hurrying to my car with a distinct sense of hope building inside me. This tome was what I needed. My intuition was practically buzzing. I couldn't wait to dive into the book and find whatever lay within that could help Tabby.

My phone buzzed with a text as I hopped into the driver's seat of my car.

It was from Damon.

How was your day, beautiful?

I ignored the "beautiful" part of his comment and answered promptly.

I didn't find anything to help Tabby in the library, but the principal just loaned me an ancient spell book, so I'll look into it when I get home. I'll keep you posted.

His response was immediate.

Fantastic. Chat soon. XO.

That little kiss and hug at the end of his message made me feel like a giddy schoolgirl. I couldn't stop staring at the screen. I reread it and analyzed my emotions, wondering if I was looking into his text too far. Regardless, the truth was I wasn't a schoolgirl. I was a schoolteacher and a woman of thirty-two years. I didn't have time for ridiculous, tummy-fluttering crushes. I had to get my head out of the clouds and focus on the task at hand. Tabby needed me, and I was finally getting closer to helping her.

CHAPTER 6
JAYDY

I spent the whole of Monday evening looking through the ancient book, and when nothing seemed perfect for the job at hand, I decided it was time to cast a spell. One that would help me find what I needed, much like a magical compass. As soon as I put my hands over the book and chanted the words of the spell to take me to my heart's desire, the pages began to flutter of their own accord. I stared down in wonder, having had no success with this particular spell in the past.

The book pages flicked back and forth between two pages as if it couldn't decide on one or the other. "Both of these?" I asked aloud, my brows furrowed as I analyzed the situation. The book began to magically shake as if to agree with me. I slid both my hands into the pages to bookmark the spells, and the book immediately quieted. "Thank you," I breathed, a thrill of excitement and hope rippling through me for Tabby's sake.

I wasn't really talking to anyone, of course, but the Universe was always listening, and I wanted to make sure it knew I was grateful for its assistance. I grabbed an old leather bookmark that lay on the coffee table next to my couch and carefully placed it into the pages that held the second spell. Once saved, I flicked back to the first page where the location spell had directed me.

I stared down at the page for a bone-knitting spell. But the ingredients... "Shit" It called for things I'd never used and didn't even know if they were available anymore. The spell also needed one-off, unique items like "the blood of a loved one."

How am I meant to do this now? Oh! The second page!

It was certainly worth investigating. I sat up straighter and pulled the book closer, sliding the bookmark into the first recommendation and opening the book up to the second suggestion. This one was for a spell, not a potion. For "putting back what was once there."

If interpreted correctly, it could be used to restore youth, beauty, and even health. But if this was truly legitimate, why didn't every witch that had ever existed use this one? Pursing my lips, I continued to read all the way to the bottom, and on the very last line, the payment portion of the deal made it abundantly clear why witches steered clear of using this spell.

The payment for the restoration was half your natural lifespan. Potentially forty years cut short, taken away forever. Tears blurred my eyes. I couldn't offer this to a girl of only twenty-one years, a *gift* that would cut her life in half.

No. I'm not doing it. I can't.

I cried after that, unable to help it. Salty tears swelled up in my eyes and made my throat hot and tight. I didn't even know Tabitha, and yet I couldn't help but feel horrible and sick for her, especially as a shifter. Could she or did she ever shift into her wolf? The image that rose to my mind of a paralyzed wolf hopelessly dragging herself around, her hindlegs unfeeling, made further sobs rise and fall in my chest until I couldn't contain it anymore and just broke down into sobs.

I needed to help her, but I didn't know how. The task felt suddenly overwhelming, frustrating, and impossible. A despairing part of me began to feel like I shouldn't have even agreed to look into this case for the handsome shifter lawyer brothers, but the relentlessly kind heart that beat at the very core of me couldn't agree with that.

My cell began to ring, startling and sobering me. I glanced down at the screen to see it was Tania. She was on her honeymoon, so what on earth was she doing calling me? I didn't have time to fetch tissues or clean myself up in a human manner, so I threw a quick spell at my face, using magic to dry up all the tears and snot. Then I answered the phone, immediately on edge. "Tania!" I gasped. "Is something wrong?" The happy laughter that came through the phone immediately erased my panic, and relief washed over me.

"Nothing! All's good here, Jaydy," the happy newlywed said.

I climbed out of my barrel chair and walked around the living room, needing to burn off the adrenaline shooting chaotically through my system. "Oh, thank goodness. I was worried for a moment. So, what's up? Have your husbands finally let you out of bed?" I snarked as playfully as I could muster. I didn't want my distress or mood to tarnish her happiness, so I did my best to sound upbeat.

She laughed again, louder this time. "Hardly! They're beasts, those two, but I just had a premonition to call you. I'm not sure why, but I always trust my instincts. Are you okay, Jaydy?"

I looked toward the ancient book with a grimace and sighed. "Well... yes and no, but you're on your honeymoon. This can wait."

But my best friend wasn't having any of it. "Nonsense! Tell me everything."

Knowing just how stubborn Tania was, I gave her a quick rundown on Tabitha, the book, and my frustration at not being able to find anything that might realistically help.

"You need to talk to my mum," Tania said immediately. "And if she can't help, I'll put you in touch with the Ancient who cursed my in-laws."

My jaw dropped, and my eyes bugged out of my head. "I'm

sorry... what? The Ancient? You *know* an Ancient?" I asked in disbelief.

"Ah... yeah," she said with an apologetic sheepishness to her tone. "I really do need to tell you that story sometime. In fact, let me convince my guys to give me a few hours respite, and I'll transport myself home. You and I can go for a visit."

I blinked, astonished.

Is she serious?

"You can transport now?" I guffawed at her. "Since when?" And exactly how much magic did my friend have now that I didn't know about?

"You just get ready to travel," she told me. "I'll be there in ten minutes."

I glanced at the clock. "But its dinner time here, and—"

"Exactly. So, we still have at least an hour of daylight. I won't be long!" Then she hung up on me to sort out affairs on her end.

I set my phone down and just stared at it. What was I supposed to be doing again?

Oh, yeah... I need to get ready!

I had no idea what *getting ready for magical travel* consisted of, but I changed out of my work clothes and into some comfortable gym leggings, a T-shirt, and grabbed a sweater in case it was cold wherever we were going. I quickly slammed down a protein shake to fill my belly, and by the time I'd finished swallowing the last sip, Tania had transported herself into my living room.

"Oh my God," I whispered as I continued to stare at her. "I can't believe you're really here, just like that. And you already look *so* tan!" She was wearing a floral maxi dress and looked as healthy and happy as I'd ever seen her. Even more so, if I were being honest.

"Thanks," she said, holding out her hand for me to take. "Now, let's get going. Have you got the book?"

I ran over to the barrel chair and grabbed it up, clutching it to my chest protectively. "I do now."

"All right," Tania said. "And fair warning... she can be a little crabby sometimes, but overall, she'll be happy for the company."

I didn't get to ask who she was talking about before Tania took my hand and used her magic to transport us out of my house. It was the strangest feeling having Tania's magic pulsing in my veins. There was nothing visible except a bright white light for a moment, then I was standing side by side with her in a dark, dusty cabin.

I shivered as a cold hand caressed my skin, but there was no one there. Looking around quickly, I noted the simple wooden furniture, wall of books, and the small fire burning away in the grate.

"There you are, girl," an old, croaky voice said from behind us.

I whirled around, clinging tightly to the book. The woman, who was clearly a witch, looked about a hundred years old.

She watched me with an assessing look.

I gulped before finding the courage to speak. "Hello. I'm Jaydy."

She nodded at me, her gaze still shrewd. "You must be one of Tania's powerlifter friends."

I would have blushed at her comment about my physicality if I hadn't been so in awe. The woman practically glowed with power. "Ah... yes. That's me."

Tania rushed forward and embraced the old witch, interrupting our little tense interlude. "It's so nice to see you, Helga!"

The witch closed her eyes for a moment, then pulled away to look Tania in the face. "How was the wedding, dear?"

"Oh, it was great," she gushed, all smiles, clearly very at ease with the old witch. "It was no fuss really. But I'm so glad we did it."

The old witch scoffed. "You and two wolf shifters! I wouldn't have believed it was possible if I hadn't seen it for myself."

Tania's eyes slid sideways to me. "I think my friend here is falling for her own pair of wolf shifters too."

I gasped at her. "That's not true! I hardly know Damon and Chase."

Tania rolled her eyes at me as if she somehow knew something I didn't. Had she had a premotion? "Yeah, right," she said, her voice full of snark.

"It's true!" I argued back, feeling suddenly insecure—or at least more than usual. "I'm not like you, Tania. Honestly, I couldn't even hold the attention of one man, let alone keep a relationship with *two* going." My cheeks burned with a blush I couldn't control.

Tania's smile didn't diminish, and she slid her gaze over to the Ancient. "Only one way to find out though, right?"

The Ancient acted without further prompting. She held up her hand and cast a light in front of us all.

The area shimmered like the swirling insides of a crystal ball, and there, in the depths of her magic, I saw myself with Damon and Chase... intimately entwined. I gulped in shock and looked away. "It can't be true."

The witch cackled like her laugh was rusty. "It's your future, dearie. I only cast what is already written. But if you sabotage your future enough, you could win, I suppose."

"Win?" I whispered back, not understanding her meaning.

She grinned at me, and I got a look at her less than straight teeth. "Yes, you could win against Fate. If you want to beat out your future, you *can*. I've seen other women do it, and you look like you have a determined streak in you. What's wrong? Two wolf shifters not good enough for you?"

I gaped at her, flustered. "What? No! They just don't... I don't... They can't possibly *like* me. That's impossible."

The witch walked to the small table in the middle of the room. "You're wrong, Jaydy. But that's not why you're here is it? I'm tired, so tell me what you need."

My heart pounded, and my stomach twisted, sick. How could that be possible? The Ancient was surely pulling a fast one on me, she had to be. I wasn't beautiful enough, young enough, or thin enough to land two brothers as handsome as Chase and Damon. My thoughts careened in a downward spiral toward oblivion.

When I looked around, desperately trying to find an anchor in the storm of my emotions, Tania's nod of encouragement had me pushing down against my shock and fear and focusing on why I was actually there. "I... ah... I need help with a healing spell. I can't find anyone else who can help."

The old witch hobbled forward, then sat down at her small kitchen table. "Go on," she nodded, encouraging me to reveal more.

Tania took a seat next to the Ancient.

Still rattled by the vision in the witch's light, I crept forward with the book clutched in my arms. "My boss gave me this book. I used some magic to help me locate two spells that might possibly help, but I can't do either." I placed the book on the table and took a seat opposite the Ancient.

The witch immediately pulled it closer. She didn't ask me which spells I meant, and yet she flicked to the two exact pages suggested to me.

"That's amazing," I gushed, struck by her power. She was seriously incredible.

"I could help with this one," she said, tapping her gnarled and twisted finger on the page, indicating the healing potion. "If you can get me the personal ingredients, that is."

"I think I can." I could ask them. Surely, Tabitha would agree if there was any hope she could walk again and live the life she'd had stolen from her?

The Ancient lifted her gaze to me again, and this time I noticed the swirl of purple in her otherwise dark, knowing eyes. "This is for an injured girl?" she asked.

I nodded. "Yes, a young woman called Tabitha. I haven't met her yet, but I wanted to be sure I could help before I got myself that involved. She's twenty-one and has been paralyzed from the waist down since she was a child."

Tania gasped softly.

I kept my focus on the witch, who was nodding.

"And this girl is a wolf shifter?" she enquired.

"Yes, she's the younger sister of the men in your... ah... vision."

The witch rose from her seat and began collecting things from around the room. She took down jar upon jar from the shelves and even went looking through the kitchen cupboards.

"What are you rummaging around for, Helga?" Tania asked with a smile, before winking at me.

The Ancient chuckled. "Lots of those ingredients you can't buy anymore—from anywhere—but I've got most of them. Give me a moment."

Incredible...

Long minutes later, she finally came back to the table, her hands full.

When she dumped them out, I openly gawked at the pile of rustic and aged treasure. "Wow."

She sighed. "The girl's physiology and the age of her injury might mean you need an amplifier in the potion."

"Like what?" I asked. "Another witch to help? Or do you mean another special ingredient?"

The Ancient tapped her gnarly finger against her lips in thought. "In this case you might need both. Ask Tania or her mother for help with the potion."

I glanced across at my friend.

Tania nodded enthusiastically, giving me her unspoken word that she would help me make this happen.

"What sort of amplifier?" I asked again, not wanting to fail in my quest to heal Tabitha once and for all. "Something like foxglove or liquid silver?" They were both known for amplifying the effects of a potion.

The witch's lips quirked up in a strange smile. "Silver? For a wolf shifter? No, dearie. Think harder."

Oh, God. This is like another interview or school exam!

"Um..." I searched my memory but came up blank. I just didn't have much shifter-related information at my disposal. "I don't know, I'm sorry."

The witch flicked the book to the second suggested spell.

I shook my head immediately. "No way. I can't offer to take half her life!"

That is not an option. It's not on the cards.

"There's a way of changing this spell," she explained, indicating the spell on the mirroring side of the page. "I think if you do this right, you'll shave maybe *ten* years off the girl's total life span, but you'll be giving her thirty to forty years of being able to walk, run, and shift."

Fear trembled through me. "I don't know if I can."

"You can," the Ancient said with a single nod. "Stop second-guessing yourself. You know in your heart that life is about quality, not quantity. A single decade is a sacrifice many would make to enjoy a life of good health with their loved ones." She stood up suddenly and wavered on her feet.

I jumped up before Tania could react and grabbed her arm. "Are you okay?" I asked, concern rising in my voice. Her skin was paper thin, but I held on to her so she didn't fall.

The Ancient stared up at me and repeated what she'd said a moment ago. "Stop second-guessing your abilities. You're far more powerful than you realize." She patted my hand as though I was the one that needed reassurance. "It's time for me to lie down. Come back soon, Jaydy. Tania knows the way." Then she disappeared, quite literally, before my very eyes.

"Thank you!" Tania called out as though the Ancient was just in the other room, and she may have been, for all I knew.

"Wow, she's just incredible," I said as I began to collect the ingredients she'd left on the table for us. I conjured up some Hessian bags and made sure to take everything the Ancient had so generously offered.

"I'll help you." Tania carefully packed everything with me. When we were finally done, she took the bags.

I grabbed the precious book and tears filled my eyes. "How am I going to do this?"

Tania grabbed my arm, her brows quirked like I was mad to ask such a thing. "Didn't you hear what she said?"

I nodded, but the enormity of the task overwhelmed me once more.

Tania set everything down and grabbed me by both arms, shaking me softly. "You can do this! And I'll help you. I promise."

When she let go, I inhaled sharply and forced myself to calm down. "Okay. Shall we go?" I suggested, though I wasn't the one with the power to do that.

Tania nodded and grabbed the bags again. "Yeah, let's go." She took my hand and again, we were blinded by white light. Then we were moving through a cold frost that tingled upon my skin. And just like that, we were once again in my warm living room.

As soon as we reappeared, I collapsed onto the sofa, hugging the book hard. I wasn't going to be getting used to that sensation any time soon, that was for sure. "That was incredible. How do you... What?"

Tania grinned at me. "I'll tell you the whole story later, but honestly, I really have to run. My guys will be going crazy by now."

"But what if I need you?" I asked, my heart in my throat.

"You can call me anytime," Tania said, putting all the bags on the coffee table for me. "And my mum is just around the corner if you need her. Even though she didn't benefit from the genie spell, she's still extremely powerful."

I took a breath and nodded slowly, trying to find my center. Tania had blown into my life tonight like a tornado, and it looked like she was going out the same way. "All right. Thank you for coming to help."

Tania grinned and crossed her arms over her chest. "Just don't forget everything the Ancient said!"

"You mean about the spell?"

Tania shook her head and looked at me pointedly. "No, I mean *everything*. You deserve to be happy, Jaydy."

I sat up straighter. "Thanks. But—"

"But what?"

I shrugged. "I'm not like you, Tania. Guys like that aren't going to suddenly think I'm sexy. Those wolf shifters don't want me. They just..."

She waited, then threw her hands up in the air. "They what? They just want you for your magic? Hardly! You're doing this for free anyway, aren't you?"

"Well..." Of course I was.

"*Exactly*. So, it's not like they're trying to seduce you so that you knock down the price."

"But..."

"So, why wouldn't they want you?" she asked again.

"Because I'm... I'm..." I gestured toward my size eighteen body. I was proud of my strength, but my size... I'd worked for years to get comfortable with it, and it was years that my ex-boyfriend had destroyed in a single day.

"Oh, stop it!" Tania rolled her eyes. "You're fucking beautiful! And I know you might not believe me but... shit." She put a hand to her right temple. "I have to go. Leo's starting to lose it. Just listen. Give them a chance. Don't push them away for the sake of it, okay? Be open with them."

"Okay," I whispered, the memory of the Ancient's vision flashing in my mind.

"Good girl," Tania said. She waved at me with a broad grin, then disappeared in a swirl of magic.

I went to the kitchen and pulled out my emergency stack of chocolate. If there was ever a night I needed the natural pick-me-up of sugar, it was tonight. I crawled into bed with a homemade banana split and the ancient book in my lap. Tomorrow, I had to tell the wolf shifters that I'd found a cure... but maybe not the magic to pull it off.

CHAPTER 7

CHASE

I'd gotten little to no work done all day and it was eating away at me. I was distracted as hell and dying to call Jaydy but was trying *so* hard to be patient and wait for her to reach out to us first. When my cell phone rang at five pm and I saw it was her, I practically jumped out of my skin with joy. "Hey!" I said, probably a little too enthusiastically. "How's your research going?"

"Good," Jaydy said, though she sounded distinctly distant. "I need to talk to you and Damon."

"What about? Tabby?" I asked, hoping that meeting our sister would inspire Jaydy to want to help us further. We'd been stupid to keep them apart so long, but in our defense, we'd been winging this entire situation from the start.

"I'd love to meet your sister," she answered. "But I think I might need to speak to you both first if that's okay?"

A lump formed in my throat and a knot tightened in my stomach. Something was up. Was she going to give us bad news? "Can you just tell me what it is over the phone?" I ventured.

"I could, but I'd rather not."

Then there was no question about it. If she'd feel more comfortable talking in person, then that's what we needed to do. "Of course. Where would you like to meet?"

"I'm heading to the gym now," she said. "So, we could meet there? Or somewhere after?"

The stress of the last few days had built up in my body, and a workout sounded like a great idea. "I'll grab Damon and head to the gym after work as well, then. Maybe we can go and grab some dinner afterward and talk about whatever you need to tell us in a more private setting."

There was silence for a long beat of time before she answered, "Sure, that works."

The wave of relief that washed over me was well out of proportion to what had transpired between us, but I couldn't keep the smile out of my voice. "Okay. Thanks, Jaydy. We'll see you there." I hung up before I said anything that might put her off seeing us, then called my brother to tell him what we were doing.

We got to the gym just in time to see Jaydy walking in the front door, gym bag slung over her shoulder.

Before I jumped out of the car, Damon grabbed me by the arm, a look of warning in his eyes. "Don't push her, okay? She's skittish as fuck. Let's just train our asses off and take her to dinner. Let's just do it by the book."

I stared at my brother for a moment, surprised by his insight, but respecting it, nonetheless. "Yep, that's a smart play. Last thing we want is her running for the hills."

We headed inside, swiped our new cards and went to the racks with dumbbells.

I stopped myself from running over to Jaydy and instead settled for a smile and a casual wave. It wasn't easy to rein myself and my inner wolf in, but I managed. A familiar face came into the gym a moment later, and I grinned. "George!"

The huge powerlifting warlock walked up to us and shook my hand. "Chase! What are you doing here?" he asked.

My gaze slid over to Jaydy, who was putting an incredibly huge amount of weight on her barbell. "Ah... we joined the gym. I think most of our pack will end up joining too, especially since Tania's married into the family now."

George's gaze followed mine and he saw Jaydy setting up to lift. He stared at her for a long moment, then cleared his throat and turned back to me. "Can I be frank?"

"Of course," I said with a shrug.

"You need to go gentle if you're going after Jaydy."

I frowned at him and almost told him that we weren't pursuing her, and that he was misreading the situation.

But Damon, who had far less of a social filter than me, entered the conversation. "How come?"

George's eyebrows climbed higher up his forehead. "Both of you?"

I shrugged again. "What of it?"

George laughed good-naturedly. "Oh, nothing. But at this rate, you guys are going to take all the best girls."

I stepped a little closer to him. "We don't mean to be stepping on any toes, George. But..."

She's our Fated mate.

George clapped me on the back with one of his huge hands that were more like bear paws. "Oh, it's not like that. Jaydy's like a sister to me, and I'm not even into chicks, if you get my drift." He winked at me.

I couldn't help but chuckle. "Oh, yeah? Cool by me."

"Then what *did* you mean?" Damon asked, getting closer too.

Some guys might find George's declaration confronting, but sexuality was very fluid in the shifting community. We didn't care which way George swung. Quite frankly, it was none of our business. If he was happy, we would be happy. It was that complicated and that simple.

The big guy sighed heavily as he took a roll of tape out of his bag and began wrapping it around his hands. "Jaydy was dating a guy—

a warlock—last year. They were together for ages, but they broke up."

"What an idiot," Damon spat.

"Why'd they break up?" I asked, agreeing wholeheartedly with my brother, but at the same time grateful to the idiot for moving aside so we could step in and claim our Fated mate.

"He cheated," George said with a grimace. "Then he moved on with someone barely legal, and I don't think Jaydy's quite recovered."

I looked over at where our beautiful, strong girl was training and couldn't stop the sigh of wonder from leaving my throat. "Who would choose another over her?" I asked, genuinely perplexed.

George chuckled. "And that's why you'll win her heart. Just keep saying stuff like that. Girls eat that shit right up." He whacked me in the chest and laughingly said, "Not that I'd know," before he went on to train.

I jumped on the treadmill to burn off some of my excess adrenaline.

We both trained long and hard, until finally Jaydy came over to say she was done.

Sweat dripped down my face, but I'd brought stuff with me to shower so I wouldn't be too disgusting at dinner. "Great," I said, wiping my brow with a small towel. "You okay if we shower quickly?" I could feel the heat radiating off me and wanted to cool down.

Jaydy smiled. "Sure. I don't usually shower here, but I'll get ready here too. See you in twenty minutes?" She walked off with a meek smile, her luscious ass swinging in her shiny black tights.

Damn... what I'd do to get my hands on that woman!

Heat surged through me, making my cock twitch with life. My hands tightened into fists at my sides. Just when I thought I'd managed to get my lust under control, she'd come over and proved to me that it totally wasn't—not by a long shot. "Fuck. I need a *cold* shower."

Damon agreed with my sentiment wholeheartedly.

So, without further delay, we took our sweaty, exhausted bodies to the showers.

I chose cold water for multiple reasons, but despite the shock, my cock was still at half-mast and was throbbing when I turned off the shower and swiftly dried off.

We still hadn't said anything to our parents or Tabby about our conversations with Jaydy, just in case there was nothing to tell. We didn't want to give them hope if there wasn't any. No one in our pack had ever asked a witch or warlock about Tabby's injuries, but I was grateful to have the opportunity to do so now. It was worth a shot, and even if it didn't work out, Damon and I would feel satisfied that we had tried every avenue available to help our poor, brave sister.

When I was dry and dressed, I walked out of the shower area to find my brother waiting impatiently. "What were you doing in there, jacking off or something?" he said in an irritated tone.

I rolled my eyes. "I wish. If I had been, then I wouldn't be dealing with this shit." I gestured to the visible lump of my groin. "Let's go."

When we walked out of the testosterone-filled locker room, Jaydy was waiting for us with a smile on her face. Her hair was still damp, but she'd tied it up into a high ponytail. She wore blue jeans and a pretty pink top.

My heart hurt as I walked towards her. Jaydy was my mate. Everything inside me screamed out that I needed to grab her, touch her, and claim her. But I used all my control to calm my wolf and managed to speak without sounding like a lovesick idiot. "So, are there any good restaurants around here? We don't eat out often."

She grabbed her bag, a picture of power and grace. "Yeah, there's an Italian place a few blocks over if you want to follow me?"

I nodded, and we all went outside, jumped in our vehicles, and drove three blocks to a pizza and pasta joint. My stomach growled as we pulled up, and once we hopped out of the truck, the aroma of garlic in the air made my mouth water and my stomach growl.

"Oh, yeah, I'm so ready for this," Damon said, walking toward the restaurant.

Jaydy walked up to the door and grinned at us. "You guys look hungry," she observed.

"Hell, yeah, we are," Damon said with a grin. "Give me all the carbs! Please."

We headed inside, and the waitresses all greeted Jaydy by name. By the time we were seated in a booth, she was looking marginally embarrassed. "I, ah, I tend to eat here a fair bit."

I sat beside her with a smile.

Damon slid into the bench seat opposite Jaydy.

I lowered my voice to a whisper. "Don't you just magic up your food?"

She grinned at me, her blue eyes sparkling in the bright lights of the restaurant. "Well... nowadays, I do a bit. But I used to come here all the time, and to be honest, I kind of enjoy the whole experience of eating out when I can. The atmosphere, the people... it's comforting."

"I totally agree," I said, lifting the menu to stare down at the delicious meals on offering.

When the waitress came by our booth, we ordered pizza, pasta, garlic bread, and drinks.

"I love how you order," I said to Jaydy with a grin, genuinely impressed at how much she wanted to eat.

Her smile faltered. "I'm not one of those girls that can live on salad. Obviously." She gestured almost rudely to her body, as if she were disgusted, then her eyes fell to the table.

I looked questioningly over at my brother.

What did I say wrong?

Damon jumped in like a dark hero. "Well, thank God for that. There's nothing worse than wanting to eat half a cow and the girl you're with orders a sad little salad with no dressing. No wonder those skinny bitches are so mean all the time. They're probably all starving."

Jaydy's head came up and she pinned Damon with her eyes. She stared at him for so long, I was sure she was going to say something, but then she seemed to relax and didn't respond further.

The waitress came back with our drinks and the mood was lost.

Once we were alone again, Jaydy got down to why we were all here. "I wanted to talk to you both about Tabitha," she said.

I fought the sudden, primal urge to slide my hand onto her beautiful, thick thigh. "You have news?" I asked instead.

She nodded, glancing between Damon and me. "Yeah, I do. Basically, long story short, I have two spells that can be used in conjunction to fix Tabby's injury, but there's a significant price that must be paid for each spell." I inhaled sharply, nodding when I finished. There was just no easy way to say that, so I ripped the metaphorical bandage off and said what I had to say, straight.

"We'll pay whatever you want. Whatever you need," Damon answered, his eyes lighting up with hope.

Jaydy frowned at me, then glanced at my brother as if confused. Then she shook both hands in front of her, crossing them over in a negative gesture. "Oh, no, no, no! That's not what I mean by a price. I don't want payment. I mean the spells literally require something valuable and personal. There's a potion that needs ingredients like the blood of a loved one and Tabitha's hair."

I shrugged. A haircut wasn't going to be an issue, and any one of Tabby's friends or our family would bleed for her any day of the week. "Well, that's easy. What else?"

That's when she pressed her lips together and placed both her hands down on the table. "The other spell is harder," she revealed. "It's designed to restore what was lost, but its payment is usually..." She trailed off, visibly swallowing before trying again. "It takes half of your remaining years in return."

My jaw dropped and my heart raced. "What? No! We can't cut Tabby's life in half! Even if she wanted that, we couldn't agree to it, not with a clear conscience."

"Exactly what I thought," Jaydy agreed. "Thankfully, I've been able to speak to an Ancient who's willing to help me. She said that I can alter the spell so it's less potent. She estimates that it'll only take ten years or so from the end of Tabitha's life, as long as I use the potion as well."

Ten years?

That was nothing in the grand scheme of things, especially the last ten years in exchange for all that our little sister had lost and been forced to endure already.

"Would she be able to walk again?" Damon asked almost breathlessly, his gaze focused on Jaydy's face with frightening intensity.

Jaydy nodded, pursing her lips with the hint of a smile. "Yes. I believe so."

The cheer that ripped through my body upon learning this news was too strong to contain, and I punched the air and whooped aloud. When people turned to look at us, I apologized to the room but couldn't wipe the smile off my face.

This is the best news we've ever heard! Our sister being able to walk again! I can hardly believe it!

Jaydy was grinning. "It's a complicated potion and it'll take me at least a week to brew."

Damon chuckled, the same palpable relief evident in his body language. "Tabby's been waiting for fourteen years. Another week isn't going to hurt."

The wave of gratitude for the woman sitting next to me was too big to contain, and I turned toward her, my heart in my throat. "Thank you, Jaydy. Thank you *so* much." I pulled her into my body and hugged her tightly. "You have no idea how amazing this is for us to hear. It's the first hope we've had in a very long time."

Jaydy put her hand on my back and leaned in, gently returning the hug in a polite manner.

Her scent filled my nostrils, and I couldn't help but let a soft growl roll through my vocal cords.

"I can't guarantee anything," she said, pulling back quickly. "And I'll need to meet her, but I think it's a step in the right direction."

"Of course," Damon said. "She'll definitely want to meet you as well."

I nodded, but didn't elaborate further. My sister would know who Jaydy was to us from the moment she saw her with us. We wouldn't be able hide our feelings nor our natural possessiveness and protectiveness. The food thankfully arrived right on time, and I groaned as I reached for a slice of pizza. "Damn, this smells good." The cheese was melty, stringy perfection and the pepperoni was seasoned beautifully with the most satisfying hint of spice.

We all dug into our meals. Jaydy didn't hold back, eating almost as much as we did. Almost. Damon and I were huge eaters. As shifters, it was natural for us. We burned calories like no one's business!

When the table had nothing left but a few strands of cold, wayward pasta and empty pizza dishes, I leaned back and grabbed my belly. "Well, that was great."

Damon shifted in his seat and nodded. "So, when can we get all the magic stuff going? Do you need to meet Tabby first? Or..."

Jaydy nodded. "Yeah, I do. The potion requires a cutting of her hair, among other things. Plus, I'd kind of just like to meet her personally and explain everything before I go ahead with the spell."

I took my wallet out and threw a hundred-dollar bill down on the table to cover our dinner plus tip. "And what can we do for you, Jaydy?" I asked seriously. "For doing this for us, for Tabby? We have money. We could—"

"Oh, no," Jaydy said, shaking her head. "I don't want payment. I just want to help, so please let me do this without a fuss."

Damon stared at me and shook his head as though to tell me to stop pushing.

"Okay," I agreed. "But if this works, you'll be able to name your price."

She laughed softly and waggled her eyebrows. "Well, I *am* a witch. What if I want your soul?"

I couldn't help but hold out my hand, palm up and say, "It's all yours."

And so is my heart.

Her smile fell, and her eyes grew wide and suspiciously shiny, as if she might cry. Then she looked away, toward Damon. "Do you think I can meet Tabby soon? Possibly tomorrow?"

I glanced outside. It was summer, so it was still light outside. "We could go tonight if you want?"

"Tonight?" Jaydy repeated, swallowing hard, taken aback.

I slid out of the booth. "Yeah, let's go now. Mom and Dad only live about twenty minutes away. Do you want to ride in our truck so we don't have two vehicles to deal with?" I rose to my feet and stood over the table, staring down at the beautiful face of my mate, flushed and shiny.

"Um... okay. Yeah, that's probably a good idea."

I hadn't expected her to say yes, so I immediately jumped into action. "Great!" I grabbed her hand, helped her up from the booth.

She stood up, her gaze casually averted.

I didn't move back. I couldn't. I was transfixed. Her breasts were so close to my chest, I could feel the wave of heat coming off her.

Shit. Shit. Shit.

"Ah... are we still going?" she asked, looking up at me as she tilted her head in question.

Heat and lust pooled in my gut, and it took me too long to realize that I needed to step away. "Oh, yeah. Sorry," I said, stepping out and letting her follow Damon to the car. My cock was frustratingly hard in my pants, but luckily, I'd put a pair of stiff jeans on, and my shirt was long enough to cover the evidence of my inability to control myself.

The twenty-minute drive will help me calm the fuck down.

Jaydy followed Damon out to the truck and slipped into the back seat.

As I got into the driver's side I glanced back over my shoulder. "Is there enough room for you back there?" I asked.

Jaydy sighed. "I'm not *that* fat."

"No! I..." I turned around more in my seat to see she was staring out the window with her arms crossed defensively over her chest.

"Hey," I said, reaching out to touch her leg, but she pulled away. "I didn't mean it like that. Anyone over five feet seems to struggle with the leg room in this thing." And she obviously was too. She had to sit with her legs tilted to the side to accommodate Damon's seat.

He quietly slid his seat forward without saying anything.

I turned back with a sigh of my own and started the truck. How was it that everything I said seemed to upset her?

Damon grabbed his cell phone and began hitting buttons. "I'll call Mom and Dad to let them know we're coming."

"Okay." I focused on driving, my mood, which was previously elated, now sour. Why did Jaydy always think I was trying to find something negative to say about her? It wasn't true and it didn't make any sense. But I didn't dare question her and draw us into another disagreement that I wouldn't win, because I didn't know what I'd done to upset her to begin with. I just hoped against hope that we'd find our way eventually.

We have to, don't we? We're Fated mates...

CHAPTER 8
JAYDY

We drove through the suburbs and out toward the properties that I'd been told were owned by the many wolf shifter families in town. I hadn't spent much time out here, mostly because everyone in the magical community avoided the area and until now, I hadn't had reason to venture out this way.

It was truly lovely. So lush, green, and spacious. Each house sat on an acre or more of land, and all featured huge backyards close to the state forest.

I swallowed hard to clear my throat amidst the tension in the truck. I hadn't meant to bite Chase's head off, but my size had always been a topic I was sensitive about. I was so used to having to defend myself or brush off cruel comments that in the heat of the moment it hadn't occurred to me that he was simply asking if I had enough leg room. Hopefully, I could lighten the mood a little. I certainly didn't want to meet Tabby with an uncomfortable aura hanging about. "I love this area," I said. "Did you guys grow up out here?"

Damon turned around in the passenger seat and smiled at me. "Yeah. Mom and Dad bought property when they got married and raised all three of us out here."

"And Tabby still lives with them?" I asked, more for clarification than anything else. It made sense that she would, considering the severity of her injury.

"Yes, but only because she's still in college," Chase answered, joining in the conversation. "Once she graduates, her plan has always been to live independently."

"We've bought her a place in town," Damon added. "It's only a two-bedroom condo, but it's in a group of four, with space to retrofit everything she needs for wheelchair access."

Before I could comment on how thoughtful and generous it was of them to help their sister fulfil her dream of independence, Damon spoke again.

His smile widened. "But we haven't had the place renovated yet... and if you're successful, we might not have to."

His excitement for his sister's potential impending good fortune was contagious. I couldn't help but laugh too as warmth bubbled up inside me. "Well, either way, you two must be the best big brothers ever to look after your sister like that. She's lucky to have you."

Chase glanced at me in the rearview mirror. "We look after our own, Jaydy."

When his gaze returned to the road once more, a shiver of longing racked my body. I didn't know why Chase affected me so much. Even the tone of his voice, the deep timbre of his words, made me long to melt into a puddle at his feet. It was a reaction I hated to admit. Just because he was a big, strong man, who had sexy eyes and a face that the angels could have carved, didn't mean I should want him the way I did. It was embarrassing and *so* wrong.

Especially since there is no way he would ever want me in the same way.

The vision I'd seen at the Ancient's house flashed in my mind, and I couldn't help but close my eyes and bite down on my lip to stifle the moan that rose. God, that had been so confronting, and a little too hot to handle. I'd never been with two men before. Hell, I'd only been with a total of five men in my entire life.

What would I even do with that much flesh and hotness?

Chase pulled the large truck into a long driveway and began to slowly drive move toward the house. "We should warn you in advance that our parents are pretty suspicious of magicals," Chase said. "We haven't actually told them about you yet. We didn't want to get their hopes up about Tabby until we knew more."

Damon sighed. "They still feel guilty about what happened to her, even though it wasn't their fault."

I nodded along, pursing my lips in understanding. "That's understandable," I agreed. I couldn't even imagine the guilt a parent would carry, knowing their child had almost died. And seeing your child become disabled would have been a difficult pill to swallow. I wondered if a part of their guilt was the regret that Tabby wasn't living the life she should have had.

Hopefully, I can do something to help her, and they can all be rid of their guilt and live happily ever after.

Despite our leads, it might be wishful thinking, but I had to hold onto hope. I would do whatever I could and give this my best shot— for Tabitha's sake.

We pulled up in front of a large ranch-style home, and my heart immediately galloped in my chest. "I know this place," I whispered, even though I was pretty sure I hadn't been here before.

"You do?" Damon asked, hopping out and opening the back door for me.

I took his offered hand, smiling as that same little electric *zing* flashed across my palm the way it had done with Chase. I was getting used to it, but it was still strange. "Yeah... no. I'm not sure. I don't think I've ever been here, but..." I glanced around at the native trees and flowers, then shivered.

That front door.

The red wood with the carving... I'd definitely seen it before. But where? In a dream maybe? A premonition? Was that even possible?

Before I could admit to something foolish, the front door opened, and an older couple walked out. They were both tall, at least my height, and looked just like Damon and Chase. One light and one dark, but both strong and fit, though they wore their years in the wrinkles on their faces.

"Hey, boys!" the woman called out, waving her hand as she took a step off the front porch. "Come on in."

Chase put his hand into the small of my back and urged me forward gently. "We won't leave you. We promise."

I wasn't sure why that made me feel more comfortable, but it did. And in these strange, foreign waters, where it felt like I was out of my depth, I needed all the life rafts I could get.

We made our way inside, and a wave of warmth and love washed over me. It felt like I was home. My own parents had died a few years back, and even now, I felt their absence deeply. Yet here, in the bright living room filled with trophies, photos, and family knick-knacks, the hole inside my chest felt so much smaller.

"This looks like an official visit of sorts, boys. So have a seat and tell us why you're here," their mom said before sitting down on the sofa.

Her husband, who was a carbon copy of Chase, stood behind her quietly like a sentinel.

Damon sat down and patted the couch cushion next to him. "Come sit down, Jaydy."

I did as he asked but then looked to their parents. "Is Tabitha home?"

Chase's mom's eyebrows lifted high. "Of course, she's in her room. Do you three have an announcement that requires the whole family?" Her smile was starting to look suspiciously hopeful.

I immediately tried to squash any assumption that I was like

Tania. "Oh, no… it's nothing like that," I said quickly. "It's more…" I glanced at Damon for help.

He turned to his parents. "Jaydy is a witch. She's a friend of Tania's, actually."

"Leo and Mason's new wife?" their mom enquired.

"Yeah, exactly. Jaydy, these are my parents."

The woman smiled. "I'm Nancy and this is Bill."

"Pleased to meet you," I managed to say, although I could already tell that Bill was prickling in the background with the knowledge I was magical.

"Why have you brought a witch home?" their dad demanded, proving my hunch correct.

"Because we asked her to help Tabby," Damon snapped at his dad, not permitting his father's aggressive attitude to go any further.

Nancy put a hand back to calm her husband. "Help Tabby? How?"

I took a deep, steadying breath. "Chase and Damon have asked me if I can find a way to heal Tabby's spine, and I'm here to ask her and you both if that's what you want."

I hadn't told the guys I was going to ask for permission, but I needed consent from Tabby herself. She may like her life just the way it was. There was no way of knowing how much of her identity was tied up in her wheelchair ability.

Nancy stood up immediately and without speaking, left the room.

Bill stared at me, his lips thin and flat. "If this is a joke…" he warned.

"It's no joke," I whispered. "I'd never joke about something so serious."

Bill turned away, but not before I saw the anger and tears in his eyes.

It broke my heart to see it. Needing a little reassurance, I glanced back at Chase.

He leaned forward and squeezed my shoulder gently.

I should have known this would be an emotionally charged event, but for some reason, I hadn't prepared myself for it. I'd been so solely focused on *if* I could perform the magic that would be needed, I'd forgotten to think about the people involved past the initial stumbling blocks.

A moment later, a beautiful girl in a wheelchair rolled into the room. She had Chase's blue eyes, but Damon's dark hair, making her simply stunning to look at. "Hello," she said with a welcoming smile. "I'm Tabitha."

I nodded and gulped, swallowing hard. "I'm Jaydy. It's nice to meet you."

"My mom said you wanted to talk to me."

I inhaled sharply and prepared myself for further emotional backlash. "Yes, I do. I'm a witch and a friend of Tania's. I teach potions at the local magic school, actually."

Tabby's eyes went wide, and she laughed. "Mom and Dad actually let you in here?"

I couldn't stop the smile that tugged at my lips. "Well... to be fair, they didn't know I was a witch."

She sniffed the air. "They knew you weren't a shifter though."

"True," I said with a smile. This girl was lovely. Her soul practically emanated with warmth. "Well, I won't beat around the bush. It's not my style."

Tabby grinned. "Yeah, it's not mine either."

"Okay then. So, I met your brothers at Tania's wedding on Saturday and we got to talking about magic. They wondered if I could help you."

"Me?" she asked frowning, then her eyebrows shot up with realization. "You mean my back?"

"Yeah... are you comfortable talking about it?"

"Hell, yes!" she said with an enthusiasm I hadn't expected. "*Can* you help?"

I slid to the edge of the sofa, licked my lips, and spoke directly to Tabby. She was twenty-one years old and should be the only one with an opinion on this. "Yes, I think I can. It's a complex injury, and I'd have to do both a spell, and create you a rather complicated potion, but I've spoken to an Ancient—they're like an elder in our community—and she's willing to help me."

Tabby rolled closer, focusing directly on me. "And by help you mean... what exactly? Will I be able to get out of this chair?"

Tears filled my eyes at the emotion bursting through me at that moment, but I blinked them away and focused on her. "If the spell works the way I expect it to? Then yes, you will."

"Oh my God," Nancy gasped behind her daughter.

Tabby pushed herself even closer to me as her interest and enthusiasm grew. "Do you mean I could just hobble around a bit? Or could I run? Does it have a timeline? Can you be really specific please?"

I admired her desire for more information, but I could also see that she was beginning to pant a little, the excitement beginning to build inside her.

I took a breath and told her the full truth. "The potion is a healing potion, designed to reverse the damage to your spinal cord and spine, and the spell I cast will amplify its effects. The spell is designed to bring back what was lost, but it's a costly one. The Ancient has shown me how to alter it, so relatively speaking, the payment required is small, but—"

"What's the cost?" Bill demanded.

I lifted my gaze, remaining as calm as possible. "It's not a monetary cost. I am not charging anyone. I just want to help," I said to make myself clear. "But the spell demands lost years to account for the quality of life gained. If I alter it to the bare minimum, Tabby will lose ten years from the end of her lifespan."

I dropped my gaze back to the girl in the chair. "I know it's a lot to ask."

"Ten years?" she repeated. "At the end of my life? When I'm old and gray and my body is failing me anyway? Yes! A thousand times yes. Sign me up. I want to do whatever it takes!"

Nancy stood and moved closer to me, brushing Damon off the couch so she could sit beside me. When she reached for my hand, I didn't stop her, and she gripped it tightly. "Are you telling me," she said slowly, "that you have the power to restore my daughter's ability to walk?"

I smiled and nodded. "Yes. And not just walk, she should be able to do everything she did before the accident. Run and dance, whatever she likes."

Nancy's sob was heart-wrenching, and she put her hand to her mouth, her eyes closing as a flood of tears coursed down her cheeks.

"Hey," I said, squeezing her hand. "Don't be sad."

She shook her head.

Bill walked over to stand beside his wife once more, offering his support.

"If this works... we will sell the house," he said. "Whatever it costs."

"No, no," I said again, shaking my head. "There's *no* fee for my work. I don't want anything. If I can help, I will. That's all there is to it, I promise."

Bill shook himself. "No, that isn't right."

"It is," I said. "I never used to be this powerful. I wouldn't have been able to do this magic even six months ago. But my friend— Tania's best friend actually, Harry—he did a spell that cost him his life." I stopped to gulp back the emotion in my throat. "He granted Tania a wish that meant that all of us big girl witches would become as strong in our magic as we are in our bodies. So as long as I keep training and working hard, I'll be able to perform amazing magic I never even dreamed of before. So please... let me do this for Tabitha. Let Harry's sacrifice mean something."

Nancy wrapped her arms around me and hugged me so tightly I could barely breathe. But I didn't care. I'd missed these sorts of mom hugs for too long.

"Mom, you're smothering her," Tabby said, pushing at her mother from where she sat.

When Nancy released me, I wiped at my own tears.

Rising to her feet, Nancy went in search of a box of tissues.

Tabby held out her hands to me.

I took both, leaning forward so she could look into my face properly. She seemed to want to ask me something serious.

"Who are you, really?" Tabby asked, quietly, almost as if in awe.

"I'm nobody," I replied. "Just Jaydy."

"Are you really willing to offer me this... miracle? For nothing?"

I laughed softly. "I can't promise you a miracle, Tabby. What I can promise you is that I will do everything in my power to help you. We have enhanced magic, a very old heirloom spell book, and an Ancient on our side."

"Thank you," Tabby whispered, her lip quivering as tears filled her eyes.

I let go of her hands and leaned forward and hugged her tightly. "You can thank your brothers if you like," I whispered to her. "They're the ones who found me for you."

She blurted out a laugh, and when I pulled away, she reached out for her brothers.

They rushed forward, hugging her and squeezing her hands. "Thank you," she sobbed several times while they consoled her.

When Chase turned around and looked straight at me, his eyes were liquid silver, and my breath stuck in my throat. I wasn't an expert, but I had to assume that his wolf shifter had come to the surface.

Bill stepped forward once more, grim determination on his face. "We need to pay you..."

I stood up and faced the large, proud wolf shifter. "I don't need or want your money. I work, and my parents..." I stopped to take a breath, "They died years ago. They left me money and their house. It's okay... honestly. I just want to help."

Bill and I shared a moment where I thought we were both about to burst into tears, but we kept it together.

Nancy came back into the room, popping the bubble of silence.

She'd washed her face and was breathing heavily. "So," she said, exhaling in relief. "What else do you need from us to make this happen?"

Taking my time, I began to explain everything the spell and potion required, all the while trying to ignore the rising *awareness* and the butterflies in my belly with Chase in such close proximity.

CHAPTER 9

CHASE

J aydy explained everything to our parents and sister. She needed some of Tabby's hair from close to the scalp for the potion, so our baby sister would be rocking an undercut for a little while. But Tabby didn't care. She would have shaved her whole head for the mere *chance* to walk again.

Jaydy also needed a blood sample from a loved one.

Tabby suggested that I be the one to provide it.

When she said that, my legs were practically swept out from under me, and I sat down with a smile, unable to speak. I loved my little sister more than anything, and the fact the feeling was mutual made me feel even better about what we were doing. An hour later, we were ready to leave, and I felt emotionally wrung out. I couldn't imagine how Jaydy, Tabby, or my parents felt.

"Night!" Jaydy called out and waved to my family as we walked to the truck. It was completely dark now, and the full moon shone brightly overhead. Jaydy stopped and stared up at the sky before getting into the truck. "Does the full moon have an effect on you guys?" she asked innocently.

Damon laughed. "We're shifters, not werewolves."

Jaydy shrugged. "Cool." Then she slid into the back seat once more. She was smiling softly and had a very happy and settled air about her.

"All good?" I asked, as I turned the ignition on.

Our eyes connected in the rearview mirror, and she sighed. "Yeah. Everything is great."

I *so* desperately wanted to take her home, to make love to her and show her we were meant to be together, but my instincts were screaming at me not to ask more of her.

Not just yet.

I pulled onto the road and drove us all back to where Jaydy had parked her car near the restaurant. We were quiet the whole ride back, but it was a companionable, comfortable silence.

When she hopped out of the truck, she had a huge grin on her face. "See you guys at the gym?"

I nodded.

Damon got out of the truck and pulled her into him for a hug.

A shot of envy hit me.

Why didn't I think of that?

A moment later he pulled away and watched as she drove off before he got back in the truck.

I desperately wanted to punch him.

The idiot laughed as if giddy. "You should have gotten out and hugged her too. *Damn,* she smells good."

I didn't hit him even though I wanted to because I was afraid I'd end up swerving us off the road, and since we'd just found a miracle, I wasn't losing my life.

Then Damon turned to me. "You know, I was worried about Mom and Dad approving of a witch being our mate... but not now."

I grinned, focusing on the road and at the thought of what had taken place tonight. "They would have supported the Fated mate bond no matter what, even if they were grumpy about it. But with what she was doing for Tabby, they'd probably demand one of us marry her."

"Yeah... maybe," Damon mused, still sounding a little worried.

We got back to our house and for the first time in years, I fell into a dreamless, content sleep. I'd found my Fated mate. My life was officially complete.

Now we just had to convince her of that fact.

Fuck.

A WEEK LATER, Jaydy finally sent the text we'd all been waiting for.

The potion is ready.

It had been one hell of a long week. It had taken everything in me not to pursue her like my wolf was demanding. Damon and I had trained at the gym every day, pushing the limits of our physical strength, just to keep our shifters at bay.

Jaydy had called us multiple times during the week but had kept it pretty *professional.* She was very focused, working full-time, training at the gym, and perfecting a potion that sounded *extremely* complicated. She'd popped over to Mom and Dad's house a few times during the week and taken a sample of my blood at the gym one day.

I was dying to tell her what we were to her, but she was so focused on Tabby, I didn't want to distract her in any way. Our happiness could wait, but Tabitha's cure was time-sensitive. We owed it to her to keep ourselves under control and ensure the spell and potion could be made and administered without a hitch.

By Wednesday night, Jaydy had finally finished preparations.

Damon and I headed for Mom and Dad's, the tension between us electric. Tonight meant so many things. The possible beginning of a new relationship with Jaydy and a whole new lease on life for our sister.

"Is Jaydy meeting us there?" Damon asked, grabbing hold of the seatbelt and gripping tightly. He was nervous. We both were.

"Yeah," I answered. "I think she's already there preparing."

We traveled in silence the rest of the way, too anxious to voice our thoughts aloud. If this worked as planned, our baby sister would resume the life that had been stolen from her, and that meant more to me than I could possibly articulate. When we pulled up outside our family home, Jaydy's little black car was already parked out front. "We've got to get her a better car," I said, glaring at the scratched side panels.

Damon shrugged. "We can, but don't you think she'd have one if she wanted one?"

I laughed, breaking tension in my chest. "Yeah, you're probably right." Buying a car was a big deal and personal. The last thing I wanted us to do was overstep before she was ready.

When we entered the house, it was still daylight outside, but there was a darkness to the inside of the house that wasn't normal.

"Hello? Where is everyone?"

Mom came rushing into the foyer hushing us, her finger to her lips. "Shh... you've got be quiet."

"Why?" I asked, though I immediately dropped my voice to a whisper.

"Jaydy brought the Ancient here and she's..."

Seeing my mother struggle to find the right words was amusing. But I couldn't even guess what she was trying to say. "She's what, Mom?"

"She's not used to all the light or noise. She lives alone and is *very* old and *very* powerful. So you two need to be on your best behavior." Then she whacked me in the chest with a dish towel like I was fifteen again, just for good measure.

I would have laughed if it wasn't so obvious Mom was nervous as hell. "It's fine, Mom," I said, taking her hand. "Show me where they are."

She led the way into the back of the house where Dad had built a large extension for Tabby when she was injured. It was an open room like a den, with multiple pieces of furniture and a TV, all set up for Tabby's wheelchair access. But the room was transformed now. Most of the furniture had been pushed to the walls, and in the center of the room was a table, set up much like a doctor's office.

Tabby lay on the table in a pair of jeans and a T-shirt, an outfit I'd never seen her in. She'd always said jeans were too difficult to get on, so she didn't appreciate them anymore.

Then it hit me.

Tabby believed this was going to work. She knew in her heart without doubt that she was going to get up off that table and walk when all was said and done.

Tears blurred my vision as hope and emotion warred within me.

Mom pulled me over to an armchair against the wall.

Damon was on my heels and practically staggered into the chair beside me. "Wow."

His whisper had me searching the room for more clues to the magic that was taking place today. In the corner was another small table, covered with a black cloth and many magical items. A large book, a purple potion, and various flowers and herbs.

Jaydy was standing beside the table, looking down at the book and running her finger over the pages. Beside Jaydy stood a small woman with tattered black clothes and long gray hair. Together, they turned to look at me.

I swallowed the gasp that rose upon seeing the venerable witch's face. She had to be a hundred years old, and Mom was right. I could see the power rippling around her.

Jaydy lifted her gaze and met mine.

My heart squeezed tightly in my chest at seeing my mate so focused and beautiful. Her giving nature and compassion literally glowed all around her as she moved toward Tabby.

She spoke to our sister, her hand on Tabby's shoulder.

My sister was shivering as though she were truly terrified, though I could see her smile. I wanted to get up and reassure her, but when I moved as if to stand, I was met with resistance.

Jaydy looked at me and subtly shook her head.

I sat back down with an understanding nod, not wanting to interfere with their preparations and risk Tabby's future.

The Ancient asked Tabby to sit up.

Jaydy helped her sit on the table while they lifted the purple potion to her lips.

The Ancient chanted softly in a language I didn't understand while Tabby drank and drank and drank, until the entire creepy-looking potion was consumed. My stomach twisted with fear for my baby sister, but I took a calming breath and forced the fear back down.

Jaydy laid Tabby down again and whispered something to her before she rushed over to us. "Hey, guys."

"Hey," I said, wanting to reach out and touch her, but controlling myself because of the seriousness of the situation. "Is everything okay?"

Jaydy nodded. "Definitely. With the Ancient here, we have so much more power, but that's not why I came over. I just wanted to warn you that you need to stay seated, okay? Even if Tabby starts yelling or screaming—whatever happens—okay?"

I glanced at Damon.

Is she serious?

Was our baby sister really going to start screaming? From what?

Pain?

And she wanted me to sit back and watch it happen...

Jaydy squatted down on her haunches and reached out for both of us, putting a hand on one of my thighs and one on Damon's.

The Fated mate buzz rippled over my skin. I forced myself not to moan with her touch and connection.

"Do you trust me?" she asked, sounding hopeful.

"Yes." I didn't hesitate.

"Of course, we do," Damon added.

"Then stay here, *please*," she whispered. "It's really important."

It took me a moment to wrap my head around what she was asking me, but then I nodded. "Okay. We will."

Tabby began to gasp and writhe on the table behind her.

Jaydy jumped up and ran back to her.

The Ancient witch was holding the book and beginning the spell.

Jaydy put both hands out over Tabby's body and began speaking the same words. Her eyes were closed, and it was clear she was speaking from the heart. She'd told us she'd memorized the spell, but it was still impressive to see her in action.

Tabby began to scream, tearing at her clothes and arching her back like a victim from an old-fashioned exorcism movie. "It hurts!" she wailed. "Make it stop. Please!"

I dug my fingers into the arms of the chair on which I was sitting, refusing to take my eyes off my sister, but remained seated alongside my brother.

The witches ignored her pleas and cries, pushing on through the spell.

The sound of cracking bones sounded in the air, and Tabby let out a scream that had me swallowing back tears. I could hear Mom to my right, sobbing softly in the arms of our father, but no one moved to help Tabby. No one disobeyed Jaydy's instructions.

"No! Oh my God. This hurts too much!" Another scream ripped through the air, then Tabby was reaching for help with her outstretched hands. "Jaydy!" she begged. "Please help! You need to stop."

Jaydy didn't stop. Her whole body was glowing with a white light I'd never seen before, and she was chanting louder.

The Ancient moved to the head of the table and placed her hands on Tabby's shoulders, holding her still while she writhed and bucked.

The spell built to a crescendo, and sweat beaded my forehead. Tabby's screams were ringing in my head, but I pressed my weight into the chair and refused to move. Jaydy had said there would be a cost for a spell this powerful, and this was mine. She could have my blood, she could have my soul... but listening to my sister's helpless screams while I sat on watching was truly a cost I couldn't bear.

Jaydy's voice reached its peak, and the white light that had surrounded her whipped into Tabby, covering her whole body before absorbing into her flesh.

Then Tabby fell quiet and still.

My heart raced, a lump forming in my throat as silence hung over the room.

Oh my God... they've killed her.

My heart was firmly lodged in my throat. I had no idea if the spell had worked. My arms dropped, as every bit of strength in my body left with the toll of such powerful magic, and I staggered forward, gripping the table, my breathing labored. Tabby wasn't moving, and I was too terrified to touch her or check her pulse.

What if we've hurt her? What if...

The Ancient didn't seem afraid or worried at all, though. She passed a steady hand over Tabby without touching her. She moved it through the air, down her chest and to her pelvis, checking the effectiveness of our healing, I assumed. Then she smiled.

That single small gave me a surge of hope, and I reached out for Tabby's arm. She was warm but wasn't moving.

"Tabby?" I whispered. "Are you okay?"

Tabby turned her head to look at me and tears filled her eyes. "I'm too afraid to move." Her lower lip trembled.

I nodded and swallowed the lump in my throat. "It's okay, I understand, sweetheart. How about I do a quick tickle check?"

She frowned at me, her brows furrowed, and her lips quirked. "Tickle check?"

As a teacher who loved working with children, I had a few tricks up my sleeve when their little hearts were burdened, or they were feeling down. I didn't explain any further, I simply moved down the table and tickled the bare soles of her feet.

A loud, strange laugh burst out of her, and she moved her feet and wiggled her toes. "Argh! Stop, Jaydy. That tickles!"

A sob fell from my lips as I rushed back up to her head. "That's a positive sign." I smiled. "Try to sit up. Come on."

Tabitha nodded, and this time she managed to sit up pretty much by herself.

I bit my lower lip, adrenalin racing through my veins as the excitement of the moment grew. "And now, try swinging your legs over the edge," I encouraged, my heart pounding.

I'd added in a twist to the spell to rebuild Tabby's lower body so that the atrophied, unused muscles would be able to hold her once she stood.

Tabby's brothers and parents were on the edge of their seats, tears in their eyes, but they weren't moving. I'd asked them to stay where they were, and they did. The request had mostly just been for the Ancient's sake. She needed to focus, as I did. They could get up now if they wanted, but I didn't take the time to stop and tell them so.

I gripped Tabby's hand as she moved her legs around so they were hanging off the table. "Stand up," I whispered, fear striking me in the heart. If this failed, she'd fall. But if it didn't...

Her arm shook but she did as I asked, sliding her butt off the table and landing on her feet. Her legs wobbled, and it looked like she was going to collapse.

I wrapped my arm around her waist and held her tight.

The Ancient stood close and offered her hand too.

Tabby grabbed Helga's hand, and with our combined strength,

she got her feet under her and stood. She was wobbly, like an adorable newborn giraffe, but she was up.

She's standing! She can feel her legs!

"Jaydy... Please..." Tabby's mom called out, her voice strangled with visceral emotion. "Can we get up now?"

I nodded, my own eyes tearing up. "Just you but take it slowly. Okay?" There wasn't any danger to the magic or Tabby now, but I didn't want them all rushing her at once in their excitement. I still had no idea how this was going to play out. At this point, I was taking this moment by moment, just like Tabby.

Nancy stood up, as unsteady on her legs as her daughter. She put out her arms, like a mom waiting for her child to take their first steps.

With a determined look in her eyes, Tabby locked her legs and was suddenly taller. I hadn't realized it before, but she was almost six feet tall, and a truly magnificent young woman.

Nancy took a step toward her daughter, tears coursing down her cheeks unchecked. "Come on, baby," she said, her chest heaving with every breath. "You can do it."

Tabby took a step toward her mother, letting go of the Ancient's hand and reaching out for her mother.

Nancy didn't rush forward—which was extremely impressive—but took another solitary step toward her daughter.

Tabby let go of my hand then, and standing completely unassisted, took another step toward her mom. She wobbled and began to fall.

Nancy laughed with joy as she rushed forward and caught her daughter, swooping her up in her arms.

Bill jumped up a heartbeat later and came up behind his wife, gathering his baby girl and wife in his arms and carrying them back to the sofa.

I stared at them for a few moments, overwhelmed with joy for everyone, then turned back to the Ancient. "Thank you *so very* much. I couldn't have done this without you." My well of energy and magic felt completely drained. I wasn't even sure I'd be able to safely drive myself home.

I'd taken the day off work and spent four hours in the gym, pumping up my strength and hoping that it would be enough to lift my magic to the point where I'd be able to handle the spell. It had been enough of a boost, just.

The Ancient smiled softly in return, clearly touched with emotion herself. "It was a beautiful experience. Thank you for asking me to join you." Then she closed her eyes and disappeared, probably going home to rest.

I chuckled to myself and shook my head. "I've seriously got to learn how to do that."

When I turned around, Chase and Damon were staring at me, pleading with their eyes. The unspoken question of "Can we go to her?" passing between us.

I gestured to the huddle of people with a tired smile. "Go for it, guys."

Chase and Damon bolted for their family, wrapping their arms around their sister and parents.

I turned away from the heartachingly touching sight, emotional and exhausted. I needed to sit down in the worst way. There was still a lot to clean up in the wake of our potion-making and spell-casting, but I didn't have the magic or energy to take care of it right now.

Damon came over to stand beside me. "Come on, Jaydy. Let's go. You look asleep on your feet."

I gratefully took the hand he offered and hauled myself up from where I rested on the table, staggering sideways as I did.

Damon caught me and held me against his body, his arms protective and supportive.

The heat and strength radiating from him made me want to fall immediately asleep. I just had nothing left to give. "Tell your mom I'll come back and clean up..." I managed, before I gently pulled away and started moving toward the door, needing to lie down before I fell down. My legs felt like lead weights and my arms were beginning to feel the same.

The family huddle immediately broke apart, with Nancy and Bill surging toward me with worried expressions. Their arms went around me, hugging me so tightly I could barely breathe. But it was so nice to feel part of a family again that tears filled my eyes. "Thank you, Jaydy. Thank you," they repeated over and over again, their gratitude and love positively overflowing.

I smiled and closed my eyes. Unsure moments passed, and I woke up with a start when they moved again, and I swayed.

Nancy began to tut. "Oh, no! You're not going anywhere, young lady. You need to rest after all that." She turned to her dark-haired son. "Damon, pick her up and take her to the spare bedroom. It's all clean and made up. She'll be comfortable there."

"Oh... I have to..." I was going to say, *go to work tomorrow*, but trailed off.

Damon scooped me up into his arms like I weighed nothing.

I didn't even have the energy to feel weird about the fact he was carrying me. I was way too heavy for that, and yet he seemed to have no problem with my weight at all.

He carried me into a dark bedroom.

Nancy was hot on our heels. She turned on a warm, dim lamp and pulled back the covers on the floral bedspread. "It's not fancy, but it's clean," she said apologetically, fluffing up the pillows.

Damon set me down gently on my feet.

I swayed like a marathon runner at the finish line and couldn't stop the hysterical chuckle that rose to my lips. I'd never felt this exhausted before in my life. "I definitely underestimated the physical toll of that spell," I admitted.

Nancy came over and pushed me gently on the shoulders. "Sit," she soothed. Then she knelt on the carpet and undid my laces, pulling my shoes and socks off.

I should have told her not to do that, that I could do it myself, but it was so nice being mothered again, if only for a moment. "Thank you." I whispered, my eyes already shut as slumber began to steal over me.

"Would you like me to help you with your clothes?" Nancy whispered.

I nodded. "Yes, please." I only had a top and jeans over my underwear, but it would be nice to sleep in less. It would feel less constricted and more comfortable.

"You boys, out," Nancy said, her voice turning into a command. Then the door shut with a soft click. She came back to me, clucking her tongue. "Those boys are *obsessed* with you."

I snorted out a laugh as she gently lifted my top up over my head, then pulled me to my feet so I could unbutton my jeans. "They love their sister and knew I was the best way to help her. It's got nothing to do with me."

Nancy slid my jeans down my legs for me.

I blindly stepped out of them, then eased myself back onto the bed. "I'm sorry... I can't open my eyes." I lay down and pulled my legs up on the bed.

Nancy pulled the blanket up over me and kissed my forehead as if I were her own daughter. "Sleep, Jaydy. You've more than earned it."

"Oh... Meg!" I gasped in a sudden panic, trying in vain to sit up.

"Who's Meg?" Nancy asked softly, pushing me back down.

"My cat... she needs her food, and I..."

"We'll sort that out for you," she said. "Are your house keys on your car keys?"

"Yes," I answered, then managed to mumble out my address. After that, words failed me entirely. The gas tank had finally gone dry. Meg would be okay to sleep one night by herself if they just fed her.

Thank you, Harry.

I'd done a really good thing today, mostly because Harry had given me and other witches like me the power to make a difference. And I would be forever grateful for him. With my final thought being one of gratitude and love, I plunged into a deep and dreamless sleep.

WHEN I WOKE the following morning, I stretched my arms above my head and rolled onto my back, wincing. My body was sore, especially my shoulders and lower back, but I'd more than earned the exhaustion and pain. Yesterday was one of the most rewarding yet tiring days of my life.

Sunlight was peeping in around the curtains, lighting up the soft grey carpet and the pale-yellow walls. I hadn't been able to see when I'd staggered in here last night, but I was so grateful for the care I'd received when I'd needed it the most. A soft grunting sound made me turn my head, and I was surprised by the sight that greeted me.

There was Chase, sleeping soundly on the bed beside me.

God, he is beautiful.

He was fully clothed and sleeping on top of the covers. He was also as far away from me as he could possibly get, sleeping on the edge of the huge mattress so I couldn't feel his presence at all.

Another sound in the room, a strange creak, made me look around again.

And there was Damon, asleep in an old rocking chair placed in the corner of the room.

I lay still, not moving, not wanting to wake either of them. Had they stayed to watch over me to make sure I was okay after the spell?

That makes the most sense. Wolf shifters are protective by nature.

I'd done a lot of reading this week, not just on wolf shifter anatomy, but also on their pack structure and other lore. And one of the main themes of wolf shifters seemed to be their love for their family and the importance of their packs and their mates.

I'd thought Chase had been exaggerating when he'd offered me his soul in return for his sister's health. And in a way, he probably had been, but he'd been serious about doing practically *anything* for his family. Then, as I did a double-take, I saw the strangest and most unexpected sight. Meg, my mischievous man-hating feline, was curled up peacefully on Damon's lap.

Damon's... lap! Not even on the bed next to me, the little traitor.

I could hardly believe my eyes. The boys must have brought her back here last night. I couldn't help but stare at them for a little longer than I should have.

Damon was the one brother I couldn't get a read on. He was just so dark and mysterious, but beautiful. He was also more than a little intense and colder than Chase. I couldn't quite figure him out. Talking to Chase was easy, talking with Damon was different.

But if Meg likes Damon, maybe there's more to him than I first realized.

Chase began to stir beside me, drawing my attention away from Damon and Meg.

I turned my head back to look at him, allowing a deep sigh to escape.

His lips twitched moments before he opened his big blue eyes and looked straight at me.

Our gazes locked, and I couldn't help the smile that spread over my lips. "Good morning," I said, hoping I didn't look too rumpled and disheveled.

Chase slid off the bed backward and stood up in a graceful move I'd rarely seen a guy as big as him pull off. "Good morning," he answered. Then he gestured to the bed. "I hope you don't mind that we stayed. After the miracle you achieved last night, we were really worried about you."

I sat up, pulling the sheets with me since I was only wearing a bra and panties. "No, of course not. Especially since you brought my Meg back with you. Thank you for that. I'm glad to see she's okay."

Chase glanced toward the rocking chair. "That was all Damon," he said, giving credit where it was due. "I stayed here with you."

Damon was up now too, bouncing out of the rocking chair to stretch his arms above his head, his back cracking with the move.

"Mom would have stayed," he said, "but she and Dad haven't left Tabby's side."

Meg pranced over to the bed and jumped up onto the mattress beside me. I took her up in my arms and she purred loudly. "Hello, beautiful girl. Aren't you a sight for sore eyes?" I cooed, then smiled broadly at Damon, happiness filling my heart. "I can imagine your parents are a bit overwhelmed right now, but they must be feeling happy, too." I couldn't think of the right word for what sort of emotions they would be feeling on a day like today.

Grief, regret, worry, ecstasy? Relief? All of them probably, and everything in between.

"They're very grateful to you," Damon said, his gravelly tone making my toes curl.

I began to fidget in bed, pain pressing into my lower belly. "I... ah, would you excuse me? I need to go to the toilet."

Chase walked around the bed and went to the door. "Of course. We'll meet you out in the kitchen. Coffee?"

"Oh, yes please." I was going to need the caffeine hit today.

Chase opened the door, and he and Damon left.

I jumped up and dressed quickly. Normally, I'd use my magic to conjure up new clothes and underwear, but my power reserves were still *very* low. I didn't dare waste the little I had on a new set of knickers. Maintaining my consciousness and ability to drive home when I was ready was my top priority. I could rest and recover properly then.

When I went looking for a bathroom, I found one just across the hall. I washed my face, rinsed my teeth, and went to the toilet. My reflection in the mirror showed the strain of the last week in the purple circles under my eyes and the paleness of my cheeks. But it was worth it.

God, was it worth it!

Seeing Tabby stand up and walk to her mother after the accident that had robbed her of her ability to use her legs had been miraculous. And witnessing her parents' sheer elation and joy had been more than my poor little heart could handle. I'd probably bought myself a friendship with this family for life, which I definitely didn't mind. They seemed like really good and fiercely loving people.

With a heavy sigh, I adjusted my clothes, feeling particularly uncomfortable in the top I was wearing. I'd been training *a lot* lately and my arms were the biggest they'd ever been. I'd have to size up simply because I was bulking up. There was a certain irony in that, that wasn't lost on me.

"Time to go," I told myself as I made my way to the kitchen. I'd had a lovely time with these amazing wolf shifters, but now it was time to get back to my life.

Just Meg and me.

CHAPTER 11
DAMON

Breakfast didn't exactly go to plan. Jaydy rushed into the kitchen like a whirlwind, with her car keys and cat perched in her arms. She had a few sips of coffee, thanked us again for our hospitality, then whisked herself and Meg right out the door.

Chase and I had planned to make her a good, solid breakfast before making plans to see her again. And preferably, now that the spell business was done with, tell her that that we'd like to date her. But unfortunately for us, she'd gotten out of Mom and Dad's house as soon as she physically could. It caught us a little off guard and in her absence, we felt crestfallen. But it'd take more than a skipped breakfast to make us give up on our Fated mate.

So, instead of moping over Jaydy, we took the day off work, choosing to spend as much time with Tabby as we could. She was alight with happiness, and the joy written all over our parents' faces was something I hadn't even realized I'd missed. The house was full of joy once more.

My parents were tough, suck-it-up people. They'd always dealt with whatever life threw at them and endeavored to make the most of every situation. But now, seeing them having recovered what they'd lost in their daughter... it was hard to explain just how much of a miracle it was for our whole family. Jaydy's magic had healed more than just Tabby's ability to walk. It was like we'd all been given a new lease on life.

That night we went to the gym to work out some of our hidden angst, hopeful Jaydy would also be there. Much to our despair, she wasn't. Even though we felt the undeniable pull and power of our bond, we didn't want to overwhelm her, so Chase and I just sent a text or two to check up on how she was, and didn't bother with pushing our dating agenda.

But by the following day, I was ready to throw all our rules out the window. My effort at keeping how I felt under wraps and remaining patient had seemingly run its course. My wolf needed his mate, and I agreed. "We need to see her," I told Chase, sitting at our kitchen counter. It was Friday night, and we both nursed a beer in hand. We should have been relaxing after a long day at work, but we were both wound way too tightly for a simple beer to take the edge off.

Chase leaned back on his stool. "I know... but it's clear she's avoiding the gym, and her texts are two words. She's trying to distance herself from us, brother."

"Why the hell would she do that?" I demanded, immediately frustrated.

Chase shrugged, raising the beer to his lips. "I don't think she wants us around."

Anger welled up inside me, replacing my usual cool facade. "Well, fuck that!" I pulled out my phone, but before I could call Jaydy, I saw a text from George.

Jaydy just arrived. You've got two hours to get your asses down here, maybe less. She looks exhausted.

I pushed the beer bottle away and grabbed my car keys without a second thought. "Let's go."

"Go?" Chase asked. "Where?"

"To the gym. Jaydy's there."

My brother didn't need to be told twice. He obviously felt the same way I did. We ran for the truck in the driveway, grabbing our gym bags from by the front door on the way through. The drive was silent, neither of us speaking. We were on edge, anticipation practically buzzing in our veins. Now that Jaydy's focus was off spells, potions, and our sister, it was time for us to move in and show her we were meant to be.

Surely, witches believe in the power of Fate too?

I stayed just at the speed limit, and we got there in under twenty minutes. Adrenaline zinged along my nerves, and my wolf shifter howled inside my mind. This was our time, the right time. I just knew it. It had to be. Without delay, we jumped out of the truck with our bags and headed inside.

Jaydy was sitting on a bench, her face pink and dotted with sweat. "Hey, guys," she said, waving from her seat at a bench, but not getting up. "How's Tabby doing today?"

My heart was pounding just seeing her. No woman had ever had such an effect on me. "She's great," I managed to say. "You're a miracle worker."

She groaned as she got to her feet with a small smile, wiping her face with a towel. "Well, I'm glad to hear it," she said. "I'm actually just heading out, I think. I haven't got any stamina for this tonight." She casually flipped the towel over her shoulder and went to move past me.

I reached out for her arm, stopping her in her tracks. "Come to dinner with us tonight."

She frowned at me, her gaze a little wary, or perhaps it was just the fatigue showing in her eyes. "Oh... I'm not sure I'm up for dinner," she apologized.

"Please?"

Chase stepped closer and intervened. "You've got to eat, especially after a workout. Our treat?"

She glanced between us, then sighed. "You're probably right. Just give me a minute to shower." Yawning, she headed off to the ladies' locker room.

George sauntered over to us wearing a roguish smile. "You guys got it bad, huh?"

I didn't bother answering him, instead deferring to what was really on my mind. "Why is she so exhausted, George? She looks like a ghost." She was still beautiful, of course, but her skin was as pale as milk, and she had dark circles under her eyes.

George glanced after Jaydy's retreating form. "She's power drained," he said simply, as if that explained it.

I stared at him then raised my eyebrows. "And?" He needed to explain that more to me. I wasn't all that familiar with magic and its inner workings.

George sighed, taking a long drink from his water bottle. "And she feels like utter crap. With a witch, or a warlock for that matter, our magic fills our veins the same way blood does. And right now, she hasn't got any."

My stomach dropped, and I swallowed hard.

Holy shit.

"This is because she helped Tabby, right?"

George took another drink, then wiped his mouth with the back of his hand. "Yeah, but don't worry, it'll come back. Magic is like water in a well. She's drained at the moment, but it'll refill."

"So, what does she need?" I demanded. "Is there anything we can do?"

He shrugged his massive shoulders. "I'm afraid not. She just needs time and rest."

Grimacing at the hard truth, I nodded. "All right, thanks, bud." I clapped our friend on the back.

"Any time," he said, before he headed off to the next step in his strong man routine.

While we waited for our mate to return, I did some weights, pushing hard to bring my adrenaline down. I needed to keep myself under control, for all our sakes, or I'd blow our chance.

And that's the last damn thing I want!

When Jaydy came back into the gym, she was wearing a soft, black cotton dress. Her choice of outfit meant her gorgeous, strong legs were on display, and the mere sight of them made me want to go down on my knees to kiss her flesh. She glanced between Chase and me, still in workout clothes.

My cheeks were burning hot, and I stood there with my hands on my hips as I caught my breath.

Meanwhile, Chase had sweat dripping down his face.

"Are you guys changing too?" she asked.

I laughed softly. "Ah, we didn't bring a change of clothes. We could swing by our place on the way to the restaurant? Unless you happen to know a really casual place around here we could eat?"

Jaydy's gaze slid down to my workout shorts, then back up to my loose tank. Her gaze wasn't judgmental, but she looked like she was starting to struggle to breathe. "Um.... I do know a diner nearby that doesn't care if we go by in gym clothes. George, Tania, and I go there all the time actually, because the burgers are so good."

"That sounds great," Chase said, grabbing his towel and wiping his face. "I'm starving." We all walked outside, and Chase nodded to our truck. "Do you want go together since it's so close?"

Jaydy glanced toward her car. "Sounds good," she said, surprising us both. She hopped in the backseat again and gave us directions to a little diner with a huge burger sign and cheerful fifties music blaring.

"Well, this is cool," I said, glancing around at the red leather booths and period-accurate black and white tiled floors.

"It is," Jaydy said with a warm, familiar smile.

When a waitress came over to seat us, she knew Jaydy by name. We all sat down and ordered the biggest burgers we could, with a wide array of sides.

Jaydy didn't order as much as us, but she was smiling and seemed happy despite feeling so drained. "So, tell me more about Tabby," Jaydy said while we waited for our meals.

"She's doing really great, thanks to you. It's like our whole family dynamic has been given new life."

She smiled softly. "I'm so glad."

Our burgers arrived in record time, and we all dug in. My stomach was twisting with hunger but finally settled down once I got some food into me.

"Will you tell us more about your work?" Chase invited Jaydy, already digging into his sides of fries.

She shrugged. "It's just like normal teaching really, but the subject is more like practical chemistry than anything else."

I leaned forward, grabbing some fries. It was clear she wasn't in the mood to be talking about work right now, so I tried another angle. "What about you and your life, then? Parents? Any siblings?"

She smiled as she took a sip of her strawberry milkshake. "My parents are gone, but I have a baby brother about Tabby's age."

"Oh, I'm sorry," I said, feeling like I'd put my foot in it. "I can't even imagine losing our parents. They're the pillars of our pack."

She shrugged, as if the pain of losing them was old but ever-present. "We're doing okay," she said. "I do my best to help my brother pay for college, and he's doing well."

I glanced at Chase, and I could see him mentally making plans to help Jaydy financially.

She must have struggled without the support of her parents.

I was dying to learn more about her. I had so many questions, but I focused on eating and shoved them down. Jaydy was already exhausted, and I had no intention of overwhelming her, though my wolf was chomping at the bit.

When we were done eating, Chase talked Jaydy into coming back to our place for coffee and a chat about future help Tabby might need.

I didn't want any of our conversations to be about Tabby, but there didn't seem to be any other way to keep her talking.

We drove back to our house, and as we got out of the truck, Jaydy gasped. "Oh my God, this place is beautiful."

I stared up at the historical home we'd spent years restoring and renovating. "Thanks. We fell in love with the house years ago, but it was in pretty bad shape. Mason and Leo helped out with some of the structural work, but we've done a lot of the work ourselves."

As lawyers who sat on our asses a lot of the day, working on our house had been a necessary physical and mental stress relief.

Chase walked ahead to open the front door for us, leaving Jaydy and me in his wake.

I put a hand on the small of Jaydy's back as we moved forward. My heart raced when I heard the hitch in her throat as we walked up and into the house.

Do we make her nervous?

I sure as hell hoped so. She had to feel something... had to be able to sense the Fated mate call like we did, surely? Regardless, tonight I was determined to tell her everything.

We went to the kitchen where Chase started busying himself. "What sort of coffee do you fancy?" he asked.

"Do you have hot chocolate? It's pretty late, and I don't want the caffeine to keep me up."

"Yeah, no problem," Chase said and got to work making her a drink.

In the meantime, I took her on a tour of our home, hoping to woo her with the large library and *massive* master bedroom—a room neither Chase nor I had ever slept in before.

We've been waiting for you, Jaydy...

CHAPTER 12

JAYDY

I'd been calling myself a fool the whole drive back to Damon's and Chase's house. I didn't even drink coffee! What was I even doing?

Why did I agree to Chase's offer?

But the moment we'd pulled up, that critical inner voice was immediately silenced. Their home was incredible. It boasted six bedrooms, four bathrooms, and a library that I absolutely fell in love with from the moment I laid eyes on it.

Damon was giving me a guided tour. It was clear he loved it just as much and had a keen eye for renovation and restoration work despite his legal expertise.

Chase eventually found us in the library.

I didn't want to leave. I was walking around the room, staring up at the floor-to-ceiling bookshelves, just lost in the beauty of it when he walked in.

Chase gently touched me on the shoulder and handed me an almost comically large red mug. "Here you go."

I gratefully took the mug and warmed my hands on the thick ceramic. Then I continued to wander around the room, drinking it all in. The whole house was simply amazing. It had high ceilings and incredible historical features. Beautiful ceiling roses, plush carpets, and timeless pieces of antique furniture. You'd never guess that the guys were wealthy just by looking at them, but after seeing their home, it became apparent their law practice was obviously doing *very* well.

"Is the library your favorite out of all the rooms?" Chase asked me with a curious smile before sitting on one of the soft leather couches.

I nodded, my nerdy and witchy heart singing. "The whole house is amazing. But this room..."

Damon laughed. "It's completely extravagant, we know, but we always figured our wife would be a bit of a nerd like us."

I turned and stared at him and my heart began to pound. I licked my lips before asking as casually as I could, "Your... wife? Do you think you'll be like Mason and Leo and just marry one woman? Is that common in your pack?"

Damon walked around the room with his hands behind his back, carrying himself with a calm and cool air.

Meanwhile, Chase remained seated.

Damon was the one to answer after several breathless moments. "We didn't think so in the beginning, because it's not actually common at all. But we thought we'd probably still live together ultimately, because the house is big enough for multiple families and kids."

"That's another reason why we've never moved into the master bedroom," added Chase. "Because neither of us are married, and the room feels like a place you live with your Fated mate."

I nodded, swallowing hard. "Fated mate... I think I've read about that somewhere in my research." I'd poured over that page actually, reading it over and over. The concept of having a cosmically divined lover sounded a little bit like a dream, but in reality, I wasn't sure I quite liked the idea of being told who I had to love.

"Research?" Chase asked, his brow furrowing. "What kind of research were you doing on wolves?"

"Well, I had to research wolf shifters for Tabby's spell, because your physiology is different than mine and other humans." I sat down on a red velvet chair near the old fireplace and took another sip of my hot chocolate, savoring the heat with a sigh. The guys were just being friendly, I was sure, but there was something in the atmosphere that I couldn't put my finger on. Something electric.

Chase shifted in his seat on the couch. "And circling back to your earlier question... yes, we do believe we're only going to have one wife between us now. Mason and Leo have explained to us just how good it can be."

"Especially when you have a woman as strong as Tania," Damon added, his gaze intense as he stared straight at me.

Jealousy kicked me in the gut, so I nodded, cleared my throat, and looked away so they wouldn't see how sensitive I was. "Tania is definitely beautiful, I agree."

Damon walked over to me and dragged the other velvet chair with him, so he could sit right beside me. Then he reached for my free hand and took it.

I didn't pull away even though my heart leapt into my throat, and my skin tingled at his touch.

"Hey, can we tell you something that might freak you out? We need to be honest. We feel we owe you that much."

"Okay, sure," I said, trying to smile and act like I knew where this was going. Surely, he was just going to thank me again for Tabby's spell? Or to ask me for something else magic-related? Another favor, perhaps?

Chase stood and walked closer.

I glanced up to look at him, and his eyes were shifting to silver. My stomach tightened, and I caught my breath.

Something is up. But what?

I pursed my lips determinedly and squeezed Damon's hand. "You can tell me or ask me anything. Whatever it is you need, I'm here."

He blinked at me, then pointed that too gorgeous smile he wore my way. "Okay... well, it's probably easiest to just say it, so here goes. You're our mate, Jaydy. We've known it from the first moment we saw you at the wedding."

I snatched my hand out of his grip and glared at him, my heart hammering my chest and my cheeks flaring with heat.

I can't believe this!

"Don't be ridiculous," I said.

What sort of cruel trick was this? Why would they taunt me after everything I'd done for Tabby? I'd really thought more of them than that, but perhaps I'd been wrong. Too trusting.

Damon's smile disappeared instantly. "I'm not being ridiculous. It's true," he said with a completely straight face.

I stood up and moved away from them both, anger clutching at my stomach. "I already told you... I'll help you with any spell you want. I'm happy to help friends in need, but you don't need to seduce me or lie to me to get it. My powers are all yours. I don't require payment or false platitudes." A lump lodged in my throat, and shameful hot tears burned in my eyes.

Damon made a strange, pained noise in his throat.

Chase reached out and put out a hand to his brother, as though comforting him. "Jaydy, the truth is that we never meant to ask you to help us with Tabby. Not that we're not grateful... but you were so dismissive of us at the wedding. You couldn't believe that we'd want to date you, so we found an excuse to get close to you... we asked you to help Tabby."

"And we're so glad we did," Damon added with more enthusiasm and emotion than he usually displayed. "You've *totally* changed her life and saved our parents from their despair. You have no idea how much good you've done!"

"But that's not why we wanted you," Chase reiterated.

It can't be true. It can't.

I'd been so sure the Ancient had simply been having a little fun, playing a trick on me by showing me the image of me being intimate with the boys.

Surely not...

I shook my head vehemently, denying the idea. It was too much. It was too crazy. It didn't make any sense. They were them, and I was me! Besides... "You don't even know me. You can't possibly think I'm your..." I couldn't even bring myself to say it, to give voice to such an insane notion.

Fated mate.

I knew what that meant. It really had been part of my research. A Fated mate was like a soul mate, someone you were destined to love, to protect, to marry. The attraction was undeniable. The shifter who heard Fate's call was practically forced into marrying *the one.*

These two beautiful, well-off, model-like men couldn't possibly believe that a woman like me was meant to be with them. My insecurities raged within me, slapping back any such possibility, refusing to see the logic and truth in what the brothers were trying to tell me.

They can't. It's insane.

"We don't think it, Jaydy," Chase said too calmly. "We know it. What do you think that shiver of electricity is every time we touch?"

I jumped to my feet and took a step away to put some distance between us. "Static?" I said, grappling for anything that wasn't *Fated mate.*

"And the undeniable attraction between us?" Chase pursued.

I put my hands on my hips and glared at him, skipping over the question. "Do you know how ridiculous we would look together? Can you even imagine? You two are super-hot... like, classically perfect hunks. There's no way anyone is going to believe we're meant to be together. We'd literally look comical at best and obscene at worst!"

Don't they know how absurd we'd appear in society?

Damon stepped forward, his face a storm cloud of anger now. "Don't you dare talk about yourself like that! You're fucking beautiful, Jaydy. And we both want you like you couldn't possibly understand."

"I don't believe you," I retorted in a clipped tone, still throwing up a shield-wall of denial. I couldn't believe them. I wouldn't. Everything and everyone in my life had told me I wasn't good enough, especially for men like these two. They deserved to be with some perfect Barbie doll. A woman who would look like a trophy on their arms, not a size eighteen powerlifter with enough padding to outlast the winter!

Damon's eyes bulged with frustration, and he began to strip, pulling his tank from his body and exposing his perfect, sculpted chest. "Bullshit." He kicked off his shoes and toed off his socks.

"What are you doing?" I asked, my mouth dropping open as he stripped his shorts and was left standing before me in nothing but tiny cotton boxer briefs that fit him like a second skin. The outline of his cock was clear, as was the thrust of his thickening shaft against the material.

He shrugged. "I'm proving to you that I want you. If you have a truth spell or something, you can use that on me. But I can't lie about my desire for you."

I put my hand out, licking my lips, my head spinning. "Stop. Just stop."

His thumbs were tucked into the waistband of his underwear when he froze.

I wet my lips again, my body already responding to the sight of the beautiful male in front of me. My nipples were tight and hard, tingling and peaking beneath my bra. "Well, in theory, let's say I *did* believe you, then how would this even work?"

Chase stepped forward. "You mean the triad? The three of us together? However we want, I guess. We'd prefer to love you together, sleep in one bed, and all that... like Leo and Mason do with Tania. But if you want something different..." He shrugged. "I suppose we can just talk about it like any other closed triad. We'll genuinely do anything to make you happy, Jaydy. So, talk to us. We're all ears."

Oh, God... they're serious.

I put a hand to my head, feeling a strange sort of stress and worry growing inside me. "Okay... say I *do* believe you. Then you're saying Fate has supposedly chosen me for you. *Me...*"

Chase walked closer to me, closing the space between us. "Yes. *You.*"

I stared up into his gorgeous blue eyes and felt mine blurring with hot tears again. "You don't understand," I whispered, chewing on my inner lip.

"What don't I understand?" he asked, his gaze searching mine.

I couldn't believe I had to tell Chase my deepest, darkest fears. But there was only one way I was going forward with this, and that was with the utmost truth. There could be no misunderstandings or rose-colored glasses involved. "Men like *you* don't date women like *me*. And even if you do, you'll just end up cheating and leaving me, just like Greg did." Hot tears slipped down my cheeks but before I could brush them away, Chase intervened.

He lifted his hands and cupped my face, brushing the tears away with his thumbs. "Whoever this man was that was stupid enough to let you go and hurt you... he will pay," he whispered.

I hiccupped out a laugh and sniffled. It almost sounded like he was serious.

Damon walked up behind me and pressed his lips to my ear. "No, we won't waste the time. He's lost you and that's punishment enough for any man." His hands slid around my waist, and he kissed the side of my neck, his lips soft but possessive.

I shivered and leaned into him, my affection-starved body screaming out for attention, even though my head was still clearly floating down the river of denial. "What are you doing?" I breathed, though it was obvious.

"Loving you," Damon whispered back, his voice husky. "Are you going to let me?"

My heart screamed at me to stop fighting them, to just go with it. Because even if it was only for one night, being with Damon and Chase would be the single most passionate, amazing, and memorable experience of my life.

When I hesitated, Chase—still cupping my face and staring at me—added his plea. "Please let us show you that we're meant to be together. With Fated mates, touch is always the best way to feel the connection. *Please.* Let us show you."

It was the best line I'd ever heard, and my poor, romance-hungry heart couldn't fight them any longer. They might not want me in the morning, but what did that matter now? So I did the only thing I could. I nodded. "Okay..." I whispered.

Chase dropped his head and kissed me hard, stealing my breath away. The taste of his lips was pure heaven, and I couldn't stop the moan of longing that rose into my mouth as he slipped his tongue in.

Damon moved his hands up from my waist and cupping my breasts, he used his fingers to tweak, twist, and torment my already achingly tight nipples.

I gasped against Chase's mouth as pleasure the likes of which I'd never imagined spilled over me.

He pulled back, staring down at me with his gorgeous blue eyes. "Come with us. We'll be so much more comfortable in the bedroom."

"Okay," I managed to say despite the ongoing distraction.

Damon's hands were still on me, and his lips were nibbling at my neck and ear.

Chase smiled and grabbed my hand. "Come on." He pulled me out of the library and up the stairs, walking me into the master suite, the largest bedroom I'd ever seen.

"Wow... this is beautiful."

"And fit for a queen, just like you, Jaydy," Chase said moments before his lips captured mine once more in a kiss that ended the conversation. There was no more time for words—only action.

CHAPTER 13

JAYDY

Their hands slid over my trembling body, and I felt as though I was lost in a feverish dream. I couldn't tell whose hands were on my breasts or whose were lifting my dress. And the truth was, I didn't care. These incredible men wanted me, somehow. I didn't understand it, but I wasn't about to argue it either. You couldn't fake the very real desire I could feel pressing into me from every angle.

I raised my arms to allow Chase to lift my dress over my head, only to hear Damon's groan of appreciation.

"I cannot wait to kiss every inch of this body," he said, his tone bordering on reverent.

I snorted out a laugh, still self-conscious. "You'll be there a while."

Damon led me to the bed, then pushed me down so I was on my back, his dark, intense eyes staring down at me from above. "I've got all night, mate," he growled before kissing me.

I wound my arms around his neck, pulling him down until I could feel his hot chest against my skin. He was *so* beautiful, and I couldn't believe he was mine for the night. It was a fantasy breathed to life, like a fairytale from the pages of a beloved book.

When he pulled back, I tried to drag him close again, but he was moving down my body, pressing kisses to my throat and blazing a path to my breasts. Which were positively bountiful, so I hoped they liked *more* than a handful.

I arched my back and reached behind my back to unclip my bra.

"Oh, yes…" Damon moaned, his gaze glazed with lust as he helped me pull the black bra from my body, my breasts falling free. "Damn, you're even more beautiful than I thought you would be." Before I could respond, Damon set his lips to my nipple, and I was lost. His hands wrapped around my breasts, squeezing and massaging them while his tongue and lips sucked and licked at me.

I threaded my fingers into his gorgeous, dark hair, holding him close, never wanting him to stop. He played my body like a devil with a fiddle.

But then he took things to the next level and slipped his hand between us, moving his fingers beneath the thin fabric of my panties.

I gasped, eagerly opening my legs further for him. My heart raced and my breath hitched in my throat in anticipation.

Oh, my God. This is really happening!

He moved down my body, dropping to his knees so he could pull my panties off and throw them across the room. Luckily, I kept my body pretty hair free, so when he pushed open my thighs to bury his face there, I didn't stop him. He set his lips to my clit, and pleasure exploded throughout my body.

"Oh my God," I gasped and arched my back, wanting him closer.

He slid his hand up and pressed into me with his fingers, seeking the heat within.

My greedy body gripped him, and my first orgasm hit me out of nowhere, plowing through me with the brute and unexpected force of a tidal wave. My whole body shivered and shook as I cried out. I'd never come that fast in my life, but it seemed tonight was going to be *all* about new firsts for me.

Chase had stripped off completely by the time I recovered and climbed onto the bed, lying down to kiss me as well.

I grabbed him and pulled down, wanting him to touch me too. I desired them both more than I could put into words. I felt electric and alive in a way that made my heart sing and my soul soar.

Perhaps Fate is real after all.

He kissed me hard, not wasting any time joining the fray. He thrust his tongue inside my mouth, and it was every bit as wonderful as kissing Damon.

Meanwhile, Damon worked his way back up my body, past the swell of my ample hips and soft belly to my breasts, toying with my nipples again.

When Chase pulled back, I was desperate for more. My first orgasm had given me a taste of what magic lay ahead for us, and I didn't care if I sounded desperate, I wanted to drown in pleasure.

I might never get this chance again...

"How do you want me?" I asked breathlessly.

Chase grinned and glanced down at Damon. "Edge of the bed?" he asked.

Damon nodded and they both moved back, then Damon grabbed me and hauled me to the edge of the mattress as if I weighed nothing at all, pushing my knees up so I was open and ready for him.

I stared up at his abs, then allowed my gaze to drift lower. His cock was flushed and hard, lying so close to me I could almost taste it.

He grabbed his shaft and leisurely ran the head of his cock over my clit, then down to my open pussy, teasing me mercilessly.

I tried to encourage him inside me, wriggling and thrusting up, but he didn't move.

"Are you protected?" he asked.

I blinked, caught off guard.

Is he talking about contraception?

"Um... yeah. I take a shot once a year to manage that. For bleeding reasons, not so much contraception... but it covers both."

He grinned. "We're not asking for our sake, beautiful. We'd get you pregnant tonight if we could, but that choice needs to be yours. We'd never take that from you."

His words were sobering, like a bucket of cold water, and I couldn't help the question that sprang to my lips in their wake. "You're really that sure about me?"

He nodded as if the answer were obvious. "We are. Aren't you?"

Holy shit. Ice bucket number two.

I couldn't have this conversation like *this*. Naked and open, with them standing over me. I'd been enjoying myself, but now I suddenly felt vulnerable and out of my depth, the heat of the moment lost. "Um... can you let me go for a second?"

He did as I asked, though his lips turned down in a subtle frown.

I shuffled up the bed, wishing my clothes back on my body. I reached consciously for my magic and found it had mercifully refilled my inner well a little. So, for the first time since Tabby's spell, I cast a dressing spell, redressing myself completely. "I... ah. I just need a minute."

The brothers looked shocked but respected my wishes, stepping back from the bed. They didn't clothe themselves, but I'd read in my research that shifters were very relaxed about nudity.

I certainly wasn't going to ask them to dress for my sake. That seemed rude—the way they acted was part of their life as wolves. Feeling completely frazzled, I ran my hands through my hair, brushing the blonde strands off my hot face. My mind was racing quickly into a downward spiral that there was just no coming back from, at least not right now.

What am I even doing here?

"I'm so sorry. I think I rushed into this," I said feebly, unable to express what I felt raging inside.

Chase nodded. "It's okay. We understand, Jaydy. No stress, okay?" And without further comment, he grabbed up his shorts and tank.

Damon, on the other hand, just stared at me as though he

couldn't believe what I was saying. There was so much pain in his eyes, it just about broke my heart.

"I'm sorry," I whispered to him, shaking my head and biting my lower lip.

He narrowed his eyes at me, the disbelief soon turning into anger. "You're sorry? I don't give a shit about the sex stuff, Jaydy. But what you're really saying is you don't want us as your mates, aren't you? That's what this is. You're saying you don't feel the bond as we do?"

He was angry now. I could feel it vibrating through him.

Chase grabbed Damon's arm, trying to calm him down. "Brother, give her some time."

"Time?" Damon demanded, turning on him. "We've given her nothing *but* time! You kept telling me to leave her alone, to not push her. You said not to tell her the truth about who we were to her. Well, *congratu-fucking-lations*, you were right. We shouldn't have pursued her at all. She doesn't even want us!"

I couldn't stop the sob that rose in my throat.

Damn it...

I'd fucked everything up. "Damon..."

But Damon wasn't listening, not anymore. He was done. He ran down the stairs, and I heard doors slamming, then nothing but silence followed.

"Where's he going?" I asked Chase, feeling tears gathering in my throat and threatening to choke me.

"Oh, he'll probably just shift and run it for a while," Chase said as he walked over and sat on the huge bed beside me. "He needs to blow off some steam and cool down."

I shuffled over to him, needing his strength. "I'm so sorry about this."

Chase put his arm around me, clearly the more rational and calmer of the two brothers. "Don't be sorry. Damon's just being a dumbass. When he's not cold and stoic, he's a hothead."

I began to cry, unable to help it. He was so sweet, so understanding. And I'd just done something so selfish... so terrible. I'd pushed them away after they'd shown me—*me*—real affection and genuine desire. And once I let the floodgates open, there was no stopping the tears.

But Chase didn't ask me to. He simply put both arms around me and kissed my hair, soothing and comforting me without words.

I cried until my eyes were sore and my face felt swollen and puffy. I appreciated his silent brand of support more than I could give voice to. I'd just been holding everything back for so long... the hurt of my last break-up, looking after my little brother and seeing him through college, getting a new job with staff who didn't exactly like me, my powerlifting gains, and then Tabby's epic, power-draining spell...

When I'd finally managed to calm down, Chase got up and handed me a box of tissues with a soft, sympathetic look. "Are you okay?"

I pursed my lips and nodded vaguely. "Can I use your bathroom?" I asked, needing cold water for my hot face.

"Sure. There's an attached bathroom right through there." He pointed at a nearby door.

I slid off the bed, stumbling toward it, heavy, as if weighed down with the burden of swollen emotions. I didn't quite understand where things had gone wrong tonight. I'd been *so* ready for them— physically, anyway. How could I have let my stupid emotions and hang-ups get in the way of my one night with them? I must be insane or seriously broken.

Maybe it's because they wanted more than one night...

And that hit the nail on the head. They wanted a massive commitment, the biggest I could give them. They wanted me for their wife, to be the mother of their children, and I just wasn't ready for that yet. I was still figuring things out for myself, still coming to grips with the influx of power caused by the genie spell. Regardless of how Damon felt, *I* still needed more time.

I heaved a massive sigh and went into the bathroom, using the cold water to wash my face and some toilet tissue to blow my nose. I looked like a complete mess, so I used a small amount of my magic to fix my face. And though I looked made up and put together, it didn't take away the hollow, empty pain in my chest.

What am I meant to do now?

When I was calm enough to go back into the bedroom, I found Chase still sitting where I'd left him. "This room really is beautiful." I said, changing the conversation to a less inflammatory topic.

He sighed. "Yeah, it is. Tonight would have been the first night we've ever slept here." Chase stood up with a twinge of a smile.

He sounded so sad that tears, once again, filled my eyes. "Chase, I'm—"

"No. *Stop*," he said, smiling softly and walking over to me. "No more apologies. We pushed you too hard, too fast. This is our fault, not yours. We're from two different worlds, and it's a lot more to take in than Damon thinks."

"But..." My lip quivered and I had to stop talking so I didn't burst into tears again. This was truly the most vulnerable and raw I'd ever felt, and no amount of clothes or blankets was going to cover up the gaping wound I'd just discovered lurking within myself. My vulnerabilities and fears of being hurt were still fresh and weren't going anywhere anytime soon.

"No buts," Chase said. He was so calm, he didn't seem to be upset at all. Quite the opposite of Damon. "To be honest, I don't think any of us truly appreciated just how much Tabby's spell took out of you. You're exhausted, aren't you?"

I nodded, and before I could stop it, another sob rose and fell from my lips.

He held me tighter. "We have a saying in our family. You aren't allowed to make any life-altering decisions when you're compromised... and you're obviously compromised, beautiful girl. You're exhausted. Physically, emotionally and, can I say, magically?"

I half laughed and half sobbed as I nodded my head in agreement.

"Then, it's not right that you had to hear us talking about the future and what we wanted. I'm so sorry."

He's sorry?

How could he be sorry when I was the one who'd fucked everything up? I began speaking with a quivering bottom lip, trying desperately to make him understand. This sort of thing just wasn't me. I didn't ever jump into bed with a man I'd just met, let alone two men who were completely out of my league. "But…"

He squeezed my shoulders and didn't let me continue, which was probably smart. Whatever was about to spill from my lips wasn't going to be coherent or particularly intelligent, I was certain. "Would you like to sleep here tonight?" Chase offered. "We'll stay in our bedrooms, of course. You can just rest, then you don't need to dredge up the strength to drive home. I can even go and get Meg for you again."

I managed a smile at the mention of Meg. I still couldn't believe my cat liked these two. That should have given me a clue that something more than professional courtesy was going on between us all. I'd always said she was an excellent judge of character.

Wrapping my arms around my body, I shook my head. I didn't want to have to deal with Damon in the morning. He would think I was a horrible, selfish, cock tease. Taking my pleasure from them, then rejecting them the first chance I got. Tears welled in my eyes again, and I shook my head. "No, thank you. I think I just want to be home tonight."

"All right," he said kindly. "I'll drive you home then."

"But my car—"

"Is at the gym, I know. But you're in no state to drive right now. I'll come get you in the morning and take you to your car, okay?" He stood and reached for my hand, guiding me to stand.

"Okay," I whispered sadly and began walking with Chase to the door. But the moment I tried to step foot over the threshold of the main bedroom, I physically couldn't. My intuition, my magic, everything inside me screamed at me to stop. *Now.* I unconsciously stepped back into the room and felt everything inside me immediately ease. I took a deep, steadying breath, examining what I was feeling. My magic didn't want me to go forward, and I couldn't understand why.

"Are you coming?" Chase asked from the other side of the door.

"Ah... yes..." I tried again but this time my magic literally yanked my knees out from under me and I practically fell to the floor, a yelp of momentary panic escaping my lips.

Chase rushed in and scooped me up, his brows creased in confusion. "What's going on, Jaydy?"

I couldn't help but laugh. "If I didn't know you guys were wolf shifters, I'd think you were warlocks."

"Huh?" Chase frowned at me, confused.

My whole body had turned to jelly on me. It was the most bizarre feeling.

He stood back and rested his hands on his hips, looking as confused as ever. "I don't get it. What do you mean?"

I stared up at him, feeling a strange amount of humor and horror bursting through the darkness of the night. "Has a warlock or witch put a spell on this room?" I asked.

Now Chase was really frowning. He looked genuinely aghast and concerned. "Of course, not! Well, not that I know of, anyway. Before Tania and you, we've *never* had anything to do with magic folks."

I nodded slowly, coming to terms very quickly with whatever this force was. It wasn't foreign then. It was my own magic.

Was it being triggered by the bond? Fate?

I couldn't even begin to guess just yet, but the result was the same, regardless. "Well then, it looks like I'm staying tonight." I'd have to ask my neighbor to feed Meg, but at least I was coherent enough to send her a message, unlike last time.

Chase's shoulders dropped and his arms fell away, immediately relaxed. His eyebrows even shot up like he was surprised, but he didn't ask any questions. Instead, he just headed to the door, accepting what I said at face value. "Do you want anything? Water? Extra blankets?"

I glanced around. The room was well fitted with a huge duvet and its own luxurious bathroom. "Just a glass of water would be great. Thank you."

"I'll be right back," Chase said, and headed off.

I stood up and slowly paced the room. I could have conjured myself a glass of water, but I needed a moment alone to think. I checked the room for crystals, talismans, or signs of a spell, but there was nothing. This really was all *me*. My own magic had turned against me. It wanted me to stay here, not just in this house, but in this room. And although I was oddly amused, I was too emotionally exhausted to figure everything out. Like always, I just had to roll with the punches.

Chase returned, seemingly having no issue walking in and out of a room I seemed to have no ability to do the same in.

I took the glass of water from him and smiled finally, my face still strangely dehydrated and wet at the same time. "Thank you, Chase. For everything."

He leaned in and kissed me on the lips so sweetly that tears swam in my eyes again. He cupped my face and smiled as though he knew what I was thinking. "I'm not giving up on you, Jaydy. This is just a bump in the road. We'll figure it all out in time." Then he bid me a good night and left me alone, closing the door behind him.

Placing the glass on the bedside table, I collapsed onto the huge bed, my head and heart a whirlwind of emotion and memories. Despite my pain, I fell asleep quickly, utterly exhausted, only for visions of Damon's disappointed face to torment me all night long.

CHAPTER 14

CHASE

My fuckwit of a brother didn't come home until the wee hours of the morning, I had to assume. I tried my best to stay awake just so I could yell at him when he returned, but once the clock ticked past 2 am, I was out.

Going to sleep in my own bedroom yet again, knowing my mate was right next door was a new type of torture. I knew exactly how she would look curled up in our sheets, on our mattress, her lush curves on display, her long blonde hair spread out like a halo of golden sunshine... all alone. I couldn't get the image out of my head and inside, it killed me. This wasn't how it was meant to be, but when was anything, really?

When I awoke sometime just after sunrise, I went looking for signs that my brother was still alive. A strong sense of relief washed over me when I found them. Being rejected by your Fated mate certainly wasn't something that most shifters had to deal with, so a part of me understood his pain. But I couldn't help but wish he'd handled it better, for all our sake.

Muddy footprints were traipsed through the kitchen and ended at his bedroom door, which was shut. It looked like he'd come home still in wolf form after having run for most of the night, only shifting back right as he retired, no doubt mentally and physically drained.

I shook my head with a heavy sigh and went back to bed. Despite my desire to get some more shut-eye, I couldn't sleep. I tossed and turned hopelessly for another hour or more. The need to be beside Jaydy and the desire to be holding her overwhelmed me. I got up, grabbed a pair of thin sweatpants, and went to her bedroom.

I shook my head at the thought. *Her bedroom.* She was in the master suite, the room we'd subconsciously reserved for our Fated mate. And she'd instinctively taken it. I lifted my hand and knocked softly against the carved door, my heart immediately drumming against my ribs. Soft footfalls sounded before the door was opened a crack, and Jaydy's face appeared. "Good morning," I said, my soul at ease when she seemed to relax upon seeing me.

"Good morning," she said in return as she opened the door wider.

I gestured to the hallway with a lopsided smile. "Do you want to come down for some breakfast? Waffles are my treat to make on weekends."

She smiled brightly. "Sure." She took a step toward the door, then fell back with a groan of frustration, unable to set foot over the threshold. "I can't!"

I scratched my head, my brows furrowing. "Ah... any idea why? Is there someone we should go and grab for you? The Ancient maybe?" Whatever was keeping Jaydy captive in the master bedroom had nothing to do with us.

She groaned again. "No. I have no fucking idea."

I grinned at her language.

She'll fit right into our family.

"Okay... well, how about I go make us some breakfast and I'll bring it to you in bed then?"

I may as well enjoy whatever time I can with her.

"Is Damon here?" she asked quietly, her eyes darting from side to side as if she could see down the hallways, even though she couldn't.

"I think so, but I haven't checked," I said honestly. "But his door's shut and the kitchen's a mess. He obviously shifted and went running to cool off last night. He'll no doubt sleep until noon."

Her face changed from relief to sadness, then back again. She was obviously feeling a lot of things after last night too. "Okay, great." She smiled and gestured for me to enter the room. "Come in. I can have breakfast here. I'm feeling better."

"Well, that's good. I'm glad to hear it," I said, walking into the room and stopping, waiting or expecting to feel whatever was stopping her from leaving. A part of me wondered if she could be faking this so that she could stay, but why would she do that when we *wanted* her to stay forever... and she'd been the one who wanted so desperately to leave?

"Are you coming over?" Jaydy called out from her place on the bed.

I chuckled and strolled forward, sitting down on the opposite corner of the bed so I could look at her. "Yeah, sorry. I was just seeing if I could feel whatever mysterious forcefield you're feeling."

"And?" Jaydy asked, her eyebrows rising high on her forehead. "Can you?"

I laughed this time. "No, not at all. Maybe our house just wants to keep you?" I joked.

She frowned deeply, little creases appearing between her eyebrows. "Yeah... something like that." Then she shook herself and sat up straighter as if dismissing the thought for the moment. "What would you like me to make? Waffles?" she asked.

I leaned back on my hands and shrugged, loving the way her gaze fell to my naked chest and roamed freely. "I thought I was making breakfast. If not, I don't care, beautiful. Whatever you want."

She grinned and began moving her hands over the space between us. Out of nowhere, a small table appeared, and upon it were plates of waffles, glasses of orange juice, a bottle of syrup, and tubs of yogurt and fruit.

"Wow," I said, staring at the food and licking my lips. "That looks so real."

She laughed at that and shook her head as if I'd said something daft. "It *is* real. Dig in! I'm starving. Do you want coffee too?" She poured syrup on a waffle and dug in, then stared at me as though she were waiting for an answer.

Oh, yeah... coffee!

"Yes, please. Cream, two sugars."

She waved her hand once more, and two coffees in takeaway cups appeared.

"Whoa... that's seriously, amazing," I said, slowly reaching out to grab the paper cup before lifting it to my lips. Half of me expected the cup to just disappear before my eyes, the same way it had appeared. Instead, the coffee flowing from the cup was smooth and sweet and almost too hot. "Perfect."

She did a happy little shimmy on the bed and began to eat in earnest.

The sound of a voice clearing behind us had Jaydy's face going pale, and me turning around to glare at my brother. My ire didn't last long, though. Damon looked genuinely terrible. His hair was all scruffy, and his chest was scratched up. He looked like he'd been dragged through a hedge backwards or worse. "Go take a shower, then join us," I called out, then turned back to my breakfast.

Jaydy set her coffee down on the makeshift table and begin fiddling with a piece of the waffle she'd only moments ago devoured so freely.

"Hey, don't let him get to you," I said, picking up a plate of waffles and pouring syrup over them. "He was an asshole last night and he'll apologize, or I'll fucking make him."

"He has nothing to apologize for," she said, too softly.

I wanted to shake her but settled for scoffing instead. "He does, and you need to know that. We're all allowed to feel how we feel. Hell, between the three of us, we've got enough strength, magic, and emotion to blow the place up... But that doesn't mean we just run roughshod over anyone. And we're definitely not allowed to hurt you. We're going to make mistakes along the way, I'm sure, and he made some last night. So, now he's got to apologize and make it right." I returned to eating and tried to keep my emotions under wraps.

When I looked up, Jaydy was staring at me with a look of wonder. "What?" I asked.

She shook herself and offered me a small smile. "I just... that's a great way to look at it. Who taught you to approach things that way?" She picked up the tub of yogurt and a spoon, waiting for my answer.

"My parents, I guess. We were always allowed to be big and loud and say how we were feeling and what we were thinking, but we weren't allowed to hurt each other on purpose. And if we did, we had to apologize and mean it. And if he thinks he's getting away with this..." A soft growl rolled through my throat.

Jaydy gave a startled laugh, her eyes lighting up with humor. "You'll what? Call your mom?"

I shrugged at the thought. "Trust me, it wouldn't be the first time." The shower was still running in the bathroom down the hall, so I knew I only had a matter of moments before Damon returned. "I have to ask you though, now that you're calmer... what upset you so much last night? Was it the Fated mate stuff, or the pregnancy things Damon was saying?"

That had been lunacy on my brother's behalf. Him telling a non-shifter that we wanted to get her pregnant and stay together forever when we barely knew her. She must have thought Damon was crazy or forcing his will on her. No wonder she'd lost any desire after that.

"Oh... ah..." Jaydy set down the yogurt and ran her fingers through her long blonde hair, her tongue darting out to wet her lips. "I..."

I grabbed my cup of coffee and warmed my hands on the cardboard. "Take your time, Jaydy. I'm not trying to rush you. I just want to help get this figured out." Though getting her to explain the real issue before Damon returned was kind of necessary.

"I don't really know," she said, then shrugged her lovely shoulders.

I moved my hand through the air in an expressive, open gesture. "Just talk it out," I suggested. "Say whatever comes into your head. It doesn't have to be right or wrong, just honest. Was it the pregnancy thing?"

Her cheeks went red, and she bit her lip. "Well... yeah. It was, I guess. But it wasn't really that..." she said, trailing off.

My patience was holding on, though I desperately wanted to reassure her that everything was going to be all right.

She just needs to tell me her fears first.

"Then what was it?" I coaxed. "What scared you the most?"

She stared at me with her big blue eyes, all shiny with more unshed tears. "Well..." she took a breath, then gulped. "I think it was the certainty you both had, more than anything. You think you want me... *Forever*. And that makes no sense to me at all. The Fated mate concept, I mean. I understand it in theory, but it doesn't mean I get it. Do you know what I mean?"

The water was turned off now and the shower pipes stopped making any noise. I couldn't hear Damon moving around, but he would be. He used his wolf shifter skills well and had always moved almost silently through the house. I tried not to worry about him turning up and instead focused solely on Jaydy.

"Well, you're not a shifter," I said, trying to show her I understood how she felt. "So, I guess it's the same for us. It's difficult for us to see it from your perspective, especially in the heat of passion like last night."

She ducked her head when her cheeks went red again, and bit her lip in a way that drove my inner wolf wild.

I just smiled at her embarrassment and forged on ahead. "For us, being Fated mates takes away all the uncertainty and guesswork from a relationship. We know from the outset that we are designed for you, so we can simply skip over all those other hurdles with confidence."

She tilted her head to the side like a cat. "What do you mean?"

I shifted on the bed, setting my coffee down so I could lie on my side and look at her. "I mean, we don't have to wonder if we're meant to be or not. Or if we're going to last the test of time. We don't have to worry about whether you're a good person, or the right fit for us, or any of that stuff. You're our Fated mate. So that makes you perfect for us—and it also makes *us* perfect for *you*."

"Perfect," she whispered, her face showing a myriad of emotions as she smiled, grimaced, then teared up.

What is going through that head of hers? Is she still worried about not being traditionally beautiful enough for us?

"Not perfect in the sense of a magazine cover or some such bull-shit," I said quickly. "Perfect as in, our flaws won't break us. Perfect as in, made for each other. It means we will work out and find happiness despite all our eccentricities and obvious issues. A Fated mate bond is a promise, and we trust in that."

She huffed out a little breath and wiped the new tears that fell onto her cheeks.

I reached out to touch her thigh, to reassure her, to create a connection, skin to skin. "My brother and I aren't perfect, not by a long stretch, Jaydy. Damon can be cold and has temper issues, and I can be flippant and withdrawn sometimes." Though I was trying my best not to let that happen with her.

She frowned at me. "You? Withdrawn? Seriously?"

I laughed. "It's true. I'll give you fair warning. But since my brother threw a tantrum last night, I couldn't go off being all sullen too, could I? One of us must try and balance the other out." That would have been the end of everything, I was sure. But Damon and I had always been in perfect balance with one another. If one fell down, the other would rise above and lift the fallen brother.

And now it's my turn to be the one doing the heavy lifting.

She shook her head. "No... I'm glad you didn't do that."

"I'm sorry we pushed you too fast. We didn't mean to, it's just…" I sighed. "We've been waiting for our Fated mate for years. So, when we found you, we just assumed that you would feel the same way. It's stupid, I know, given you're a witch and not a shifter, but it's what we thought, right or wrong." I threaded my fingers through my hair and sighed again. That was the honest truth.

"And that's why Damon got upset last night?" she asked, then gulped. "Because I wasn't certain? Because I got scared about all the *forever* talk?"

"Probably," I answered. "You'll have to ask him yourself. I'm not a mind reader, even if we do share a strong brotherly bond. I can only ever guess what Damon's feeling." The floor creaked behind us, and I turned to look over at my brother.

He was creeping into the room, fully dressed in jeans and a T-shirt, but he looked pale.

I sat up and swiveled around, getting closer to Jaydy so she'd know I was there for support if my brother decided to be an asshat. I raised my eyebrows at him, but before I could demand that he say something helpful, he took action all on his own.

He walked over to Jaydy's side of the bed and went down on his knees. "Please forgive me," he said, his voice husky and thick.

Well, that's a first.

Jaydy glanced at me.

I smiled, nodding back at my brother. "Go on. Talk. Open communication is the only way any of this is going to work."

Jaydy turned back toward him. "It's okay, Damon. You can get up."

Damon didn't so much as budge an inch. "No. You need to know that I'm truly sorry for ruining last night."

"You didn't ruin last night," Jaydy interjected. "*I* did. I got overwhelmed, and scared, and I just… I guess I panicked."

"You reacted like a normal human. Or non-shifter," I said, reaching out to hold her hand. "It's not your fault we were so… enthusiastic."

Damon nodded. "Chase is right. It's not your fault. I shouldn't have told you all those things. There's no way you could have possibly been ready so soon."

Jaydy sobbed a little, her gaze finding the sheets.

Damon made a keening noise in his throat and plowed ahead, undeterred but clearly determined. "I'm sorry, Jaydy. Please forgive me for making you feel so uncomfortable and rushed. But don't leave us, please. I'll do almost *anything* except leave you. Just tell me what I can do to make it up to you, and I'll do it, I swear."

"Hold me. Please," Jaydy whispered,

Damon got to his feet immediately and slid onto the super king bed, opening his arms to her without hesitation.

Jaydy launched herself at my brother, tears falling down her cheeks.

Damon wrapped his arms around her, offering her his quiet, dark, and moody strength.

I sat back and watched them cling to each other like long lost lovers who had been apart for too long. With a wobbly smile, I picked up my coffee and took another sip as Jaydy sobbed against Damon's chest. The emotions in the room were far too heightened, and I was struggling to breathe.

Then taking me completely by surprise, Jaydy reached out and grabbed my hand and tugged, wanting me closer too.

The tightness around my chest immediately lifted, and I crawled over, leaning in, and pressed my head to hers before kissing her cheek.

Jaydy let out a long sigh that had all the sadness around us melting away with pure relief. She wasn't giving up on us, and we weren't giving up on her.

We just have to give her a genuine, heartfelt reason to stay...

CHAPTER 15

DAMON

Holding Jaydy in my arms after the night I'd had was like a dream come true. I'd been *so* angry about her reaction last night. Then, it hurt so much more when her words and confusion had finally registered.

This morning, when I woke up alone, cold, and dirty, I'd seriously thought my life was truly over. A frigid, dark chill like a shadow of despair from the void had taken over my body and encased my heart. I had no idea how I was going to face my life knowing my mate had rejected me. And not just me, but she'd rejected my brother and the life we could have given her if only she'd trusted us.

Then I'd heard them... Jaydy and Chase, chatting and laughing. I'd been certain I was experiencing an auditory hallucination, but I wasn't. It was very much real, and the sound of their good cheer had forced me to drag my ass out of bed. Instead of an empty master suite, I'd been greeted by the scene of my brother eating breakfast in bed with our mate.

In our bed.

Our super king bed... the bed we'd consciously never slept in before because it was where we were meant to bond with our mate.

Together. Anger had surged through me until I met Jaydy's startled gaze. She looked pale and seemed fearful of my return. Chase hadn't slept with her or made love to her after I'd left, that was clear. I didn't know what *had* happened, or why she'd chosen to stay, but I'd ask them when the opportunity arose.

I kissed Jaydy on the top of the head, my lips on her golden hair as I inhaled her heavenly scent.

She pulled away, wiping at the tears on her cheeks. "Are you hungry?" she asked meekly.

My stomach growled loudly in response to her question, as if daring me to lie to her, but that was something I wasn't prepared to do. "Yeah. I am."

She gestured for me to join them.

"Having a picnic?" I asked, striving for a light tone.

"Yeah... I can't leave the room, so I foresee a lot of bed picnics in my future." She half chuckled to herself as she waved her hand over the space in front of me and conjured up a plate of waffles, more syrup, and a decadent platter of fruit. "There you go."

"Thanks." I managed to say, breaking my awed stare to glance over at my brother, then back at her again. "Ah, sorry... you need to back up a step. I feel like I've missed something. You can't... what?"

Did she just say that she can't leave the room?

Jaydy picked up her cup of coffee and shrugged. "I tried to leave last night, and again this morning, but I can't walk over the threshold."

I stared at her, then at my brother, then back again to my mate. Adrenaline began zinging its way along my veins, and I couldn't stop the smile that spread so easily over my lips. She seriously couldn't leave our house? Our master bedroom?

What a pity that is....

Jaydy snorted and shook her head, rolling her stunning eyes at me. "You should see your face right now," she remarked.

I tried not to grin, but I couldn't help it. I must have looked like the most stereotypical male in existence. "Sorry," I said half-heartedly, "but that's kind of the best thing I've *ever* heard."

She rolled her eyes again, but I saw her smile behind the plate of waffles.

With a bounce in my heart's step and a healthy appetite to boot, I dug into the food Jaydy had summoned for me. I ate the whole plate of waffles, breaking up the sweetness intermittently with bites of fresh strawberries. "This is great, thank you. It's really hit the spot," I said, then ventured to ask the question I'd been dying to ask the entire time I'd been eating. "So... do you know why you can't leave the bedroom? Was it the Ancient? Or another witch maybe? Assuming the reason is magic, of course."

Who would be casting spells for us except Jaydy? Is Tania home from her honeymoon? Is she conspiring to get us all together? It's a nice thought, but...

Jaydy sighed. "I think it's *my* magic, to be honest."

"Your magic?" I asked, interrupting her. That sounded like the best possible reason I could think of.

She bit her lip and continued, "I can't control what it's doing. This isn't on purpose or anything. But it seems like my magic wants me to stay. I just don't know why though."

My heart hammered against my chest, and I glanced over at my brother, hope swelling painfully in my chest. I'd made a total ass of myself last night and I didn't want to say the wrong thing this morning when things were working out, even if tentatively so far.

Go on, brother. Talk! Tell her we want her to stay. Forever.

Chase plucked a strawberry from the platter. "Do you think it might have something to do with the fact we're Fated mates?" he asked casually. "Maybe your magic wants us all to sort out what went wrong last night?"

I couldn't have put it better myself. Thank you, brother!

Afraid that I'd fuck everything up again, I returned my attention to my meal and bent my head to finish off the last few bites of waffle left on my plate. The tension in the room mounted as the silence stretched. The hair on the back of my neck stood on end. I cautiously lifted my head, afraid that Jaydy may be reacting poorly or be getting ready to run.

And yet she literally couldn't even if she wanted to, I realized. That made me feel immediately uncomfortable. All jokes and sexual innuendo aside, I wasn't happy she was trapped here. That would be a terrible fate for anyone, but especially for someone with a strong spirit like hers.

Before she could answer Chase, I slid off the bed and walked to the doorway, stepping over the threshold, then back into the room again, testing it.

"Are you leaving?" Jaydy called out, her voice tainted with worry.

I wandered back to the bed. "No, I was just... checking. I guess I just don't like the idea of staying in the room if you're feeling unsafe and trapped. I don't want you to be worried about me or my wolf when you have nowhere else to go."

Jaydy's blue eyes sparkled as she sat up straighter on the bed and smiled at me. "That's lovely of you to say and thank you. That kind of opens us up the things I wanted to talk about."

"Like what?" I asked, grabbing the armchair from the corner of the room and dragging it over to the bed so I could sit near her, but not crowd her.

She smiled and reached out a hand to me.

I squeezed her fingers and frowned at her as I held her hand in mine. "Are you okay?" I pressed.

She nodded, her throat working as she held my gaze. "Yeah... more than okay. You're just so thoughtful."

I didn't respond. Truth was, I didn't know how. What could I say to that after what I'd done last night? I'd been the opposite of thoughtful. I'd been a selfish, immature fuckhead. I'd misplaced my anger and let my fears get the better of me. Wanting to do the right thing, I pushed away the shame that threatened to overwhelm me and faced my mistake head on. "I need to apologize again and explain what really happened last night."

She turned her whole body toward me and nodded. "Okay, Damon. Whenever you're ready. Take your time."

I squared my shoulders and swallowed the lump in my throat, grateful for her patience. "I hope you didn't think it was because you stopped us during sex, because that wasn't it. You can *always* hit pause or say 'no', that's not even a question. Chase and I will always respect your bodily autonomy."

She smiled. "I appreciate that, but it's okay. I assumed there was more to it than that. I know there was for me."

Thank God.

Jaydy really was so damn reasonable, which only made me look like an even bigger dickhead. "Okay... good, I'm glad." I took another deep breath and forged on.

Open communication. You've got this.

"So, the main problem and why I blew up, was because I thought you were rejecting me as your mate. I thought that you didn't feel the same way about us as we felt about you, and the mere thought killed me."

"Well, I—" Jaydy began.

I shook my head, interrupting whatever she was about to say. I needed to get this out before she side-stepped what we were talking about, or said something that wasn't the truth just to make me feel better. Despite the pain, I preferred to hear the truth.

"You don't have to explain anything, and that was my mistake. You aren't a shifter. You don't have the absolute confidence that comes with a Fated mate bond. We grew up with the lore. Our parents are Fated mates. It's always been a possibility and a part of our lives. So, I guess what I'm trying to say is I'm sorry for scaring you with the intensity of my feelings. I didn't mean to. I was trying to reassure you, more than anything. And I—"

"It's okay," Jaydy said, sliding her warm hand over my arm.

I swallowed down the thickness in my throat and tried to hold onto any patience I still had remaining. I needed her to listen, to understand. I couldn't have her hating me, I just couldn't.

Jaydy sat back and heaved a massive sigh. "I understand your panic and the way it must have seemed to you. I can see now that I overreacted, and I'm *so* sorry. We don't have anything like Fated mates in our community, and what you guys were saying just sounded so…"

Chase chuckled. "Crazy?"

She grinned and nodded toward him. "Yeah, kind of. But I can see that for you both, it's, well, normal. You're completely comfortable with the concept of Fate choosing your mate for you. Why on earth would it choose me, I still have no idea, though. And that's the part I'm struggling with the most, I think. I mean… you could be wrong… right?"

"Wrong?" I repeated, blinking at her.

And she thinks we're the ones that're crazy. Ha!

Chase gestured to the tray and all the food as if trying to bring the heavy conversation up to a more lighthearted level. "Should I take this to the kitchen now, or…"

"All good. Just leave it," Jaydy said, glancing at my plate. "Everyone all done?"

"Yep," I answered.

Chase nodded in agreement.

She snapped her fingers, and it all disappeared like it had never existed in the first place.

I gaped at the now empty space between us. "Now, that's cool."

That is going to take some serious getting used to!

Chase slid closer to Jaydy and put his hands on her thighs.

She didn't shrink back or respond negatively, which told me a lot about their comfort with each other.

Amazingly, I didn't feel a surge of jealousy at all. Instead, it seemed to calm me more. I'd assumed we'd lost her completely last night, so if Chase had managed to talk her down and gain her trust, then he did more than I could have, and I owed my brother my thanks. I shook myself. "Hey, so can we go back to the whole *you could be wrong* thing? What do you mean by that?"

She leaned into Chase and sighed. "I mean exactly what I said, I suppose. Can't you both be wrong? What if I'm not the one for you and you're both just distracted or confused because of Tania's wedding to her set of brothers, or whatever?"

I ran a hand through my tangled hair, holding onto my patience by a thread. I hated that Jaydy felt so insecure about herself and what she had to offer. She was beautiful, smart, strong, and kind and that was just scratching the surface! Whoever destroyed Jaydy's confidence deserved to die.

Chase slid behind Jaydy and put his arms around her. "Sweetheart, I know you are looking for a reason to think that we might not want you, but why? I have no idea. But we *do* want you, and we'll wait as long as you need to be comfortable with that fact."

I glanced up at Chase, my heart in my throat.

He avoided looking at me in return. He knew that I'd die from frustration if she continued to reject us. But there was always the gym, runs through the forest, cold showers, and beer...

I took a slow, deep breath, needing to get my head on right. I'd let my emotions blow up everything between us last night and couldn't let it happen again. I refused. No matter how badly I felt, or how my chest ached, I had to keep my shit under control. So, as best as I was able, I gathered my thoughts and pushed forward. "So... what do we do about getting you out of here?" I asked, standing up to walk off some anxious energy. I could keep my tone cordial, but the restlessness in my legs meant I *had* to move. Then a thought suddenly occurred to me. "Meg! Is she okay?" I gasped, turning to our mate, my eyes wide with worry.

I know how much she loves that cat!

Jaydy giggled to herself and smiled, as if touched by the thought. "Yeah, she should be fine. I sent my neighbor a message to feed her, though I'll have to do something else if I can't go home soon." She was still smiling at me, her blue eyes sparkling as though she were amused.

I had to ask. "What?"

She shrugged. "I guess I just can't believe Meg actually likes you. She normally hates men. She's very wary of them."

My lips twitched as I tried not to smile. "Well, she has good taste in men, obviously."

Jaydy stared at me for a long time, her bright gaze assessing and thoughtful.

It made me want to hide. But I stood still, letting her look as long as she needed. This was about making sure Jaydy was okay. I was on home turf. She was at a distinct disadvantage, and I wanted her to feel as safe as possible, given the strange situation in which we found ourselves with her magic.

"Well... let's see if our talk has fixed anything," Jaydy suggested as she slid off the huge bed and walked toward the door.

I held my breath.

She tried to step into the hallway, and stood there frozen like a statue, then turned and huffed back. "Nope. The magical block is still there. It's like walking into an invisible wall."

I laughed, because how could I not? "Wow, you really weren't kidding."

She crossed her arms over her massive breasts and glared at me playfully before rolling her eyes. "Of course I wasn't! I wouldn't lie just to stay here with you. If I wanted to stay, I'd just say so. I don't need to pretend I can't escape."

I walked towards her. "You know, I wouldn't mind if you did." I slid my hands tentatively around her waist, once more holding my breath as I waited to see what her reaction would be.

This time she melted into me. Her hands slid up my chest, and she lifted her chin as if she wanted to be kissed.

I didn't act on my immediate desire to grab her and kiss the life out of her. Instead, I simply enjoyed the feeling of her being in my arms again. It felt so damn right, there was no way it could be wrong.

Jaydy smiled at me, her lips pursing before she spoke. "You guys said that the best way to feel the connection was to... um, have sex, right?"

I nodded, gulping down the lump that formed in my throat.

Oh, shit… no way.

"Yeah," I answered hesitantly.

She went a little red in the face then nodded. "Okay."

"Okay what?" I asked, scarcely daring to hope.

Chase walked up to us so that the three of us were together.

Jaydy's warm gaze slid from Chase to me, then back again. "Okay… let's finish what we started last night and see if I can feel this incredible mating bond you're talking about."

Relief sailed through me on swift wings. It was like all my birthdays had come at once. I bent my head to kiss her luscious lips.

Best. Day. Ever.

CHAPTER 16

JAYDY

I shivered with longing, my entire body aching with anticipation.

Damon dropped his head and kissed me. His lips were soft and lush as they brushed against mine. I'd expected someone like Damon to be rough, to practically force my lips apart and plunder my mouth, stealing my breath away and leaving me dizzy, but he took his time, slowly increasing the pressure, his strong hands wandering as he seduced me into responding.

And respond, I did. I couldn't help it. Everything inside me cried out for him and so I lifted my chin, seeking a deeper connection.

He moaned and pulled me closer, right into the cradle of his hips and the growing hardness there.

I slid my arms around his neck, letting out a breathy groan. I wanted them *both* so much, it was overwhelming. I yearned for them more than anyone or anything before in my life. They were like a drug I'd only had the smallest taste of, and already I was addicted.

Their desire for me still made no sense, given just how absolutely gorgeous they were, nor did the fact they thought I was their Fated mate. I couldn't help but feel they could both do so much better than me. In fact, it seemed painfully obvious, but my magic wanted me to finish what we'd started last night.

The only way it seemed that I was getting out of here was to feel what I needed to feel and experience what I needed to experience. And after that, well, I guessed we could all go our separate ways if that was the path we needed to follow.

For now, though...

A gasp left my lips, surprising the hell out of me as I reacted instinctively to another touch.

Chase's hand slid into my waistband, and he pushed my leggings down over my hips and the swell of my ample ass, then down my thick thighs.

Damon broke off our kiss, inspired to further action, and helped his brother undress me.

Together, they tore off my T-shirt and made short work of my underwear. And too soon, I was standing there completely naked, exposed, vulnerable, and aching in every conceivable way.

"It's your turn," I said with a smile as I bit my lower lip, stepping away to watch them both strip. I'd seen them both naked last night before everything had gone to hell in a handbasket, but I hadn't savored the moment the way I should have.

I will today.

I'd consciously etch their beauty into my mind and hoard the memory forever, keeping it safe to warm me on the cold nights I would no doubt face in my future. With an internal shiver, I shook off the thought and forced my mind back to the present.

No looking forward or back.

Chase, my beautiful light-colored angel, only wore jeans, which he quickly removed.

Damon, my dark demon, took a little longer, but when they were finally both naked and standing before me very obviously aroused, it was like the whole world stopped and shrunk to a single pinpoint in time—this one.

I had to taste them I realized, as a deep sense of carnal desire welled up within me, aching from my very core, before spreading like wildfire through my veins. I'd never been bold in the bedroom, but instead of talking myself out of it, I took a step forward and went down on my knees between them. Now was not the time for fear or doubt. The three of us were committed, and I was not going to be the one to deny the magic sparking between us like fireworks in a star-spangled sky.

They both just stared at me in wonder, their lips parted and jaws slack as they drank in the sight of me.

I waved them forward, allowing my inner strength to bolster me and give me the courage I needed. "Come closer, please," I requested, my voice coming out in a husky whisper.

Damon stepped up first, right next to my left shoulder, bold as brass for all three of us, his gaze blazing with sensual hunger.

I reached for his thickening cock, wrapping my hand firmly around its girth.

Damon hissed with pleasure, and the sound made my body pulse with need.

"Closer," I whispered, staring up at him with big eyes while gently drawing him forward by the cock.

He stepped even closer, until he was within reach of my lips.

Damon groaned long and deep as my lips enveloped him, and his open and honest expression of ecstasy made my pussy clench with need. His cock was thick and silky soft, but also *so* hard. He felt hot and tasted salty and masculine in all the right ways.

Just perfect.

Keeping my hand wrapped firmly around his shaft, I turned my head to reach out for Chase, who was too far away. I made a small, plaintive sound of desire, licking my lips slowly and seductively without breaking eye contact, making my intentions abundantly clear.

My light-colored wolf shifter stepped up, his beautiful eyes glittering.

I wrapped my hand around him and sighed with satisfaction. His cock wasn't quite as thick as Damon's, but it was equally as perfect.

So delicious...

I couldn't stop myself from wiggling over on my knees to draw him even nearer as I sucked the arrow-shaped pink head into my mouth. He tasted just as amazing as he looked. On my knees, before two men who could easily be Paris-bound male models, I felt like a naughty little girl in a candy store.

Keeping my hands on both men, I moved my palms up and down in tandem, all the while sucking first one, then the other. A heady sense of power and pleasure raced over me as my tongue danced over them. They wanted me, both of them. It was beyond incredible, no matter which way I looked at it.

Damon growled suddenly and stepped back out of my grasp.

I wanted to ask what was wrong, but there was no need.

The way he was panting and gripping his cock as though to stop himself from coming, spoke volumes, certainly more than words ever could.

"More?" I asked Chase, glancing up into his beautiful blue eyes. Just because my dark wolf was done with this part of our playtime, didn't mean my light wolf was.

Chase simply smiled, his gaze flitting to his brother.

"Bed," Damon demanded, his voice almost a delicious and barely controlled growl. "Now."

Biting my lip, I hopped up and made an embarrassingly girly squeal as I raced to the bed. Jumping onto the mattress, I instinctively laid on my back, my head resting on the pillows as I prepared myself for what was to come.

Damon came to me without hesitation, crawling onto the bed and prowling straight over the top of me like a sexy, sleek predator. His shoulders were huge and blocked out the light as he dropped his head to kiss me.

I gasped, the sound lost to his lips.

He lifted one of my thighs, sliding between my legs as he bent my knee up, and his hard cock pressed against the entrance to my body.

An overwhelming need to feel him inside washed over me, shaking me to my very soul, but he wasn't moving. I thrust my hips at him in wanting and whispered with pleading eyes, "Please, don't stop."

As if he had what he'd been waiting for my final consent, he rolled further on top of me, pushing up with his hands so he could stare down upon me.

I lifted my other leg, opening myself wide as I reached up to cup his face and draw him down for another core-quaking kiss.

Without warning, he surged down, kissing me intensely as his thick cock pierced me, cleaving my body open for his.

I cried out against his lips, lifting my legs higher to wrap them around him, encouraging him into me even deeper.

He lifted his head and grunted. "Are you okay, beautiful?"

I nodded, digging my nails into his huge biceps as the intensity of our passion burned through me. "Don't stop."

I'll die if he stops now!

"Never," he whispered back, capturing my lips as he surged forward, filling me up until I didn't know where I began, or he ended.

I cried out at the sensations rippling through me, throwing my head back into the pillow and screaming at how right our union felt. Again and again, he impaled me on his perfect cock and with every thrust, a new wave of pleasure burst inside me. My nipples ached and tingled, and my belly tightened with every sexy undulation of his hips.

His cock was made for me.

Everything about it was perfect. It was the perfect length, perfect width, and he felt amazing inside me. It was like we were two pieces of a jigsaw puzzle that were always meant to be together.

Damon began to move faster and harder, thrusting like a dark, deviant demon of lust and pleasure as he chased his own release while simultaneously pushing me toward my own.

I called out to him by name, unable to stifle my cries. My orgasm was building fast, impossibly forceful and rapid, like the lead-up into a great and epic crescendo—and we were the instruments of our own blissful melody.

With a strangled growl, Damon thrust deep inside me once more, burying himself to the hilt, and came, the pulses of his heat pushing me over the edge and into the dizzying throes of the storm with him.

I shuddered and screamed out with pleasure, overcome as I rode the wave of my ecstasy like a woman possessed. It sizzled through me, searing every nerve and inch of flesh as Damon held me in his arms.

He kissed my hair as he waded through the tide of his own pleasure and whispered sweet nothings against my ear.

When I'd finally stopped shaking, my cheeks were hot, and my belly continued to convulse.

Damon kissed me once more, trailing his tongue across my lips before he rolled off me, leaving me feeling undeniably incomplete.

But how is that possible?

I'd never come so hard or enjoyed sex that had been *so* good. I couldn't want more, surely? How could what we'd just shared be topped?

Then Chase walked up to the side of the mattress and stared down at me, his eyes swimming with emotion and raw desire as he smiled the most charmingly handsome smile I'd ever seen.

That's when I realized what was missing. Chase was the third part of this incredible puzzle. Whatever magic was going on between us wouldn't be complete until I'd shared myself with both men who were deemed by Fate to be my mates. I held out my arms and gestured for him to come to me, a smile playing on my lips.

Round two, here I come!

He slid onto the bed, lying beside me and cupped my face. "Are you sure about having us both in one night?" he asked, his voice thick with compassion. "I can wait."

My heart lurched in my chest at his purity and nobility, and the world tipped sideways all over again. In answer, I pulled him down, capturing his lips and kissing him deeply. His lips were like sweet honey, his passion light and tender.

His hands went to my enormous breasts, teasing my over-sensitive nipples and cupping my flesh.

I moaned as my hand encircled his cock, tugging on his flesh with need until he was hard and thick again in my palm.

"Do you want to try getting on top?" he suggested.

Biting my lower lip, I hesitated. There was something distinctly vulnerable and confronting about riding cowgirl. It meant everything was on display and there was nowhere to hide.

"I'd love to see your gorgeous breasts bouncing and taste them while I'm fucking you."

Despite my body insecurities, how was I going to say no to that? He desired me just like his brother did, and who was I to argue with how they felt? "Okay," I said as I sat up on the bed.

Chase rolled onto his back, his entire body ripped with lean muscle.

Gods, he so beautiful.

Shoving my trepidation aside, I slung my leg over his waist, mounting my light shifter.

He grinned up at me as he filled both his hands greedily with my breasts, massaging them in his grasp, appreciating their size and abundance, his cock hard against my ass.

I eased myself up onto my knees and then slid back, grabbing his shaft before guiding it to the slick opening of my pussy.

"Oh... *yes*..." Chase groaned as our flesh connected.

Lined up, I slid down on top of him, impaling myself on his cock as if throwing myself upon a sword. I gasped as he filled me, my sensitive, already fucked insides stretching once more to be filled and accommodate my second wolf.

"Good girl," Chase crooned, sending shivers through me as he took hold of my voluptuous hips.

I raised myself up, then sank down on him once more, completely unashamed of the ungodly moans of pleasure slipping from my lips. I couldn't respond to him the way I wished I could. I wanted to tell Chase how good he felt inside me and how drop-dead hot he was, but I found talking during sex impossible, loving that Chase was able to. Everything he said, the praise and pet names, was so much hotter to me than they had any right to be.

Buoyed by his ardent admiration, I began to move faster, using my strength to ride his cock, all the while watching his face for sensual cues.

He groaned and gasped out in pleasure, even gritting his teeth and closing his eyes against the intensity of the ecstasy we shared.

I felt like a sex goddess, Chase's moans and reactions only serving to push my confidence higher and higher.

"Damn. You're so perfect, Jaydy," he managed.

I smiled with carnal satisfaction and threw my head back, arching my spine and thrusting my breasts out for his attention. My hair hung down my back, brushing across my sensitive, hot skin and heightening every one of Chase's touches. "Oh... *fuck*..." I moaned aloud.

Chase grabbed my hips, planted his feet on the mattress, and began thrusting up into me, alleviating some of the effort on my part. "God, your pussy is so fucking perfect. I'm going to come way too soon," he lamented.

With every word, my belly tightened, and my aching core began to grow hot with pleasure until I could scarcely bear the fire inside me. "Don't wait," I whispered, begging him, though I wasn't sure if he heard me. I was too close already, the beginning of the end was here. I'd get one more minute if I was lucky before I was going to come all over him.

My legs began to shake, and pleasure gripped my insides as I clutched as him like a lifeline. Chase's cock was hitting all the most perfect spots inside me, and I was hurtling towards the edge of the cliff. There was no turning back. I screamed out as magical white lights flashed inside my head, dancing through my consciousness. My whole body trembled with rapturous ecstasy and locked down.

Chase's cry as he came sounded so far away. It felt as if I were floating amongst the stars, high beyond the earthly realm, totally free and empowered. Then with startling clarity, I was slammed back into my still convulsing body. Breathless, I fell forward onto Chase's chest, the beat of his heart thumping against my ear in a familiar and comforting rhythm.

"Oh my God," I whispered into his sweaty skin, my eyes closed as I focused on exactly what I was feeling. "This is it. This is what I've been looking for all this time."

All my life I'd dreamed of this... of being loved for who I was, unconditionally and completely, and I'd finally found it in Damon and Chase. It was unbelievable.

My very own pair of perfect shifters!

CHAPTER 17

CHASE

Jaydy practically passed out on top of me after the most earth-shattering orgasm of my life. She'd professed our connection was what she'd been looking for all her life.

Those words had rocked my world, sending my soul soaring, and as my cock slipped out of her, there was nothing between us but sweat.

She felt the bond!

Damon came closer, leaving the chair he'd been sitting in beside the bed, then eased himself down to lay next to us. He reached out and rested his hand on the small of her back.

We took our time enjoying the moment together, just the three of us, when Jaydy began snoring.

Damon grinned and rolled onto his back, arms flung out like he was the most satisfied man in the world. "Well, that was fucking amazing."

Jaydy didn't stir and remained fast asleep, despite our blossoming conversation.

I put my hands on her and settled into the bed, making myself more comfortable. "I know," I agreed. "I mean… I expected sex with my mate to be *incredible*, but that was so much more."

Damon sighed heavily, a blissful expression on his face before he spoke again. "Yeah. So… when do you think Mom and Dad could put the wedding together?"

Eyes wide, I lifted my head off the pillow and glared at Damon like he was a fucking lunatic.

What the fuck is he thinking?

"Shhh!" I hissed at my brother. "You want to scare her off again?" I casually ran one of my hands through her hair and covered her ear with my resting palm.

If she's heard what he just said and freaks out again, I'll fucking kill him.

Damon frowned at me and sat up, his brow furrowed. "I didn't mean to upset her last night, you know that."

"I do," I answered, struggling to get a handle on my breathing. My heart rate had kicked up a notch as a vein of panic surged through me. "But you need to calm the hell down. The *only* reason Jaydy was still here this morning is because by some twist of Fate, her magic prevented her from leaving. We might not get another chance to show her the truth." Not to mention the fact that I'd worked my ass off to fight back my inner wolf who yearned for her, to be the sensitive guy she'd needed.

Damon grunted and slid off the bed, obviously still annoyed.

I am too, damn it.

We could have lost Jaydy last night, all because Damon couldn't control his fucking temper or his need to make this all happen on his terms. Jaydy had been hurt and needed time. He seriously needed to recognize that.

Damon pulled on his jeans and shirt again. "I'm going to go get Meg."

"Yeah, you do that," I grunted back at him.

My brother growled at me under his breath and left our bedroom.

I softly growled back, just to let some of my pent-up emotion out, but part of me was actually glad he was doing something constructive. Meg wouldn't have liked being home alone last night, considering how close they seemed, and we still weren't sure if Jaydy's magic would let her out of the room today. So bringing her fur baby to her was an excellent idea.

A large part of me selfishly hoped she'd be trapped here with us forever, but of course, I saw that feeling for what it was—ridiculous. She had a full-time job to go to every day, friends, and a gym she loved.

But maybe just for today I can have her lie here on me and sleep.

We lay there for God only knew how long, and I stayed awake the whole time, determined to just enjoy and appreciate every second I spent with my mate.

When Jaydy finally did wake for a moment, she just slid off my chest, curled into a ball, and pulled me to her.

I grabbed the thin blanket from further down the mattress and pulled it up to cover us both. Then I happily spooned her luscious, strong body, closed my eyes, and allowed myself to fall into the darkness along with her.

I woke to the feel of soft paws kneading my arm, and a sandpaper tongue licking against my chin.

"Oh... Meg!" Jaydy cried happily, the expression on her face just priceless as she rolled onto her back to cuddle the purring black furball.

"Hey, kitty," I said with a smile, petting Meg on the head before rolling out of bed to use the adjoining bathroom. I went to the toilet and washed my hands and face before returning to find my brother sitting on the bed, the cat curled up in his lap again. The sight wasn't one I'd ever expected to see, let alone twice.

He must have caught my smirk. "What are you laughing at?" Damon asked.

"You and a cat." I shook my head with a lopsided smile and climbed back onto the bed.

"Thank you for going to get her, Damon," Jaydy said as she snuggled into me again. "I think it's amazing too. Meg doesn't usually like anyone except me, generally speaking, and she *hated* my ex."

Damon snorted, petting the cat on his lap. "Well, like I said before, she has good taste."

There was silence for a moment before Jaydy spoke again. "Do you think I'll be able to get out of the room today?"

I slid off the bed and indicated toward the door. "Do you want to try your luck?"

She nodded and as she moved, clothes materialized on her body, obscuring my view of her gorgeous, larger than life form.

I sighed. "I wish you'd stop doing that. You're so perfect naked. At least give a guy a last moment to appreciate!"

Jaydy shook her head, her lips pursed. She didn't answer, instead walking to the door and stopping there.

"Is it still there?" I asked.

She glanced back over her shoulder with a spark of trepidation. "I don't know…"

"Well, go on," I said, encouraging her as I swallowed down my own fear, unsure if I wanted her to succeed or not.

Jaydy inhaled sharply, as if steeling her nerves, then walked over the threshold like it was any other door. She burst into laughter and swung around to grin at us, her face full of relief. "Well, looks like that answers that, then!"

"What does what?" I asked. I liked to think of myself as a relatively intelligent guy, being a career professional and all, but I had no idea what she was talking about when it came to magical matters. My experience was extremely limited on the subject.

She gestured to us with her hand in a sweeping motion. "Obviously, my magic wanted me to stay so we could work out what was going on here."

I laughed and stood up from the bed, my heart racing with hope. "So you believe us now? That we're meant to be together?"

Jaydy blushed prettily, then ran her fingers through her long hair. "Well, I definitely felt it," she admitted. "So, it seems like it, doesn't it?" She walked back into the room, a lightness in her step.

Damon strode over to her, his absolute adoration for our mate written all over his face before he gripped hers and kissed her deeply.

She moaned softly and followed her newfound trust and instincts, pulling him to her without hesitation.

I didn't move. I just watched, assessing my own instincts. And once again, my wolf was all good. This woman was *our* mate, and I didn't mind sharing her with my brother. It was meant to be. Our inner wolves recognized the Fated mate bond for what it was—a three-way connection.

When she pulled back, she was breathing hard, her cheeks flushed with color.

"So... what are we doing today?" I ventured, wondering if climbing back into bed with her was a possibility.

Jaydy smiled at me as though she'd read my mind. "Well, I have to train. I'm feeling much better and I have a competition next weekend, so I need to do a few hours today."

Damon sighed. "And we have the pack gathering tonight."

"Oh... shit, yeah," I said. I'd almost forgotten.

"Pack gathering?" Jaydy asked, her eyes lighting up as she seemed to fully embrace our unique witchy-wolfy world.

I glanced at Damon, chewing on my lower lip in thought.

He nodded.

The gathering would be the perfect place to stake our claim and let the rest of the pack know we were taken. "Yeah, it's the monthly gathering," I explained. "Would you want to come with us? It's all casual, of course."

She scratched her head as though thinking. "Um... Well, I have to do some exam preparation for my seniors, and then there's the gym, but could I join you after? Is it for dinner or..."

"Yes," Damon said, walking over. "Everyone brings food. It's a bit like a potluck thing."

I could see she was considering saying yes, so I added my own two cents. "Mom and Dad would love to see you. Tabby will be there too."

Her smile grew, lighting up her beautiful face. "Then count me in. Just let me know what time and where."

"Around six," I said. "And I'll send you the address."

"You don't want to stay for lunch?" Damon asked, sliding his hand around her waist once more, ever the dark and suave one.

She giggled and stepped out of his arms. "If I stay for lunch, I'm never getting to the gym. And since I can actually leave..." With a smile over her shoulder, she waltzed out of the room.

I grabbed my jeans. "Time to start the day, I suppose."

Damon didn't respond, but he was already dressed, so he walked after Jaydy with the cat in his arms.

I owed him an apology... *maybe*. I was still mad at him for last night's drama, but that would likely fade since we had now secured our mate and convinced her of our Fated mate bond. I followed them out and we said goodbye to our beautiful mate. The day had started off awkwardly, but tonight would end with all three of us in bed.

Fate willing.

I floated through the rest of the day, my feet never touching the ground. My gym workout was rather lackluster, but I didn't care. What did it matter if I missed a day or two, anyway? The competition was next weekend, but it was honestly just for fun. I loved being powerful and fit, but the competition element of it was more for distraction, and growing friendships within my training groups.

Now that I had Chase and Damon in my life, things felt distinctly different. My priorities felt like they'd shifted. I wanted so badly to see them again, and soon. And why wouldn't I? Thanks to them, my body was so blissful that every single inch of my skin was still tingling with their love.

I enjoyed a late lunch, luxuriated in a long shower, and then took a short nap to refresh myself before dinner. When I checked my phone, I found that Chase had already texted me the address of the pack meeting. According to my map app, it was a good hour's drive outside the city. Not wanting to be late, I got ready early. I fed Meg, then dressed in my favorite jeans, a white blouse, and packed a sweater.

I whipped up two delicious pies that I could share with Chase and Damon's parents and then picked up some beer as well. Thanks to my pre-planning, I left right on time. The last thing I wanted was for them to be waiting on me. I personally hated that.

The map app, as it turned out, was wrong, and I pulled into the parking lot in under forty minutes. "Well, that's unusual," I said, shaking my head at my phone.

Better early than late, though!

It was only 5:40 pm, but there were already heaps of vehicles in the parking lot. I was in the right spot. There were large trucks parked everywhere, and families were already setting up their picnic spots and working together to start a large bonfire.

I sat in my car and just people watched for a while. The adults were all laughing and drinking, while cute and healthy kids ran amuck everywhere. There was nothing that indicated they were wolf shifters to the untrained eye, but I could still tell. The men were huge, strong, and athletic. There was not a beer belly to be seen. Their metabolisms burned hard and fast from what I understood. Being a shifter required a large intake of calories, and the act of shifting, of being inherently magical, obviously utilized every last one of them.

Suddenly, my gaze caught a familiar face. "Tabby," I said to myself with a smile.

She looked amazing. The young woman was laughing and waving at people as she passed through the crowd.

People were stopping to hug her, and they all looked generally pleased to see her.

I couldn't help the rush of pride that filled me with warm fuzzies that came with knowing that I'd given Tabby back the use of her legs. She seemed incredibly happy with her newfound freedom, and it made my heart glow. Checking my phone one last time, I couldn't see any further responses from Chase or Damon, so I gathered up the pies and the beer and hopped out of my car.

The air was alight with energy, and the scent of BBQ hung tantalizingly in the air. "Perfect," I said as I inhaled deeply. It was going to be a beautiful evening. Even though Tabby had disappeared, I'd thankfully seen the way she'd gone, so I locked my car and picked up the food to venture forth into the crowd.

People moved out of the way as I weaved my way through the picnic area, smiling at the women politely, while avoiding the odd looks I garnered from the men.

A huge guy left his group and unexpectedly stepped in front of me, blocking my path.

"Excuse me," I said without too much thought as I tried to step around him.

He stood firm, blocking my path once more. "What are you doing here, witch?" the snarky wolf shifter growled at me. He was at least as tall as Damon, probably bigger, and he had a mean looking glint in his dark eyes.

Momentarily startled into silence, I took a step back, more than a little surprised by his sudden vehemence and the fact he'd picked up on my magic so fast.

He took a threatening step towards me when I didn't answer immediately.

Standing tall, I held my ground and lifted my chin so I could look him in the eye. I didn't want to show him that I was afraid or put out by his behavior, that wasn't the way to deal with bullies. In my experience, and I had plenty being a big girl, you had to be strong and stand in defiance of their aggressive and dominant position. "I'm just looking for some friends," I said casually, keeping my tone light, and even managing a smile.

Despite my outward demeanor, my heart was pounding. I had to calm myself. I knew instinctively that I could wipe the floor with this guy if I resorted to my magic, but I didn't want to drop anything, nor did I want to start off on the wrong foot with my mates' pack and introduce myself with unnecessary violence.

The guy's gaze slid down my body.

The way he was assessing me made me want to cover myself

with both arms. It was as if he could see right past my clothes to my bare form beneath. I knew he couldn't, but it made me feel uncomfortable all the same.

"Well, you aren't welcome here," he practically spat. When I didn't move, he grabbed me roughly by the arm.

Despite my newfound toughness, I squeaked in shock and pain. "Let go of me."

A growl sounded behind me.

The shifter confronting me flinched and stepped away, releasing his grip.

I turned around in relief, expecting to see one of my men, but it wasn't Chase or Damon.

"Bill... you know we don't allow witches here," whined the guy who'd confronted me, his tone much less certain now.

Bill came around to stand in front of me, then he pushed the other wolf shifter in the chest hard, knocking him back a full foot. "This isn't just any witch," he growled. "This is the witch who gave my daughter back her legs! She's the one who gave my mate back her only daughter."

His voice was filled with passion I'd never heard before, and the hairs on my arms literally stood on end in response. My heart still hammered in my chest as I watched the spectacle before me unfold.

"I... didn't know," the idiot stammered.

"Touch her again, Matthew, and you'll pay for it."

Bill's final growl sent a shiver through my whole body, and I couldn't help but chuckle as the dickhead retreated. "Thanks for that," I said to the man who'd been nothing but standoffish since we'd first met. "I probably should have waited for the guys to arrive, rather than venture into the fray by myself."

Bill turned to face me, his eyes glowing silver with his inner wolf. "I owe you too much to every repay, Jaydy. The least I can do is keep you safe until my sons arrive."

I fought back the tears at the intensity of emotion I could see glowing in his eyes. It felt incredible to feel so loved and protected by my mates' father, especially since I'd lost my own. "Thanks, Bill. Appreciate it."

"Can I take these for you?" He reached for the beer that I was still juggling.

I nodded gratefully. "Yeah, thanks. I'll hold the pies."

"No problem," he said. "This way."

I cleared my throat awkwardly amidst the stares I was getting from all those around me. My cheeks flushed with heat, but I followed Bill to a picnic table where Nancy and Tabby were already set up.

"Hey..." I said with a lopsided smile.

"Jaydy!" Tabby cried as she jumped up and hugged me tightly.

I couldn't believe how beautiful the glowing girl before me was, but I was very conscious of my grip on my baked goods as I teetered in her affectionate embrace.

"How about I take those now?" Bill said, swiftly taking the pies from me before I dropped them.

"I'm *so* glad you're here," Tabby cried, then pulled back, her eyes glistening with happiness and unshed tears. "My brothers didn't say anything about you coming tonight."

I shrugged apologetically and hugged Nancy as she came in to hug me too. "I'm sorry about that. I thought they would have told you."

Nancy pulled back and cupped my face like only a mother could do. "You're always welcome, Jaydy, anywhere we are—for all time."

I grinned to stop myself from bursting into tears.

That was the most beautiful thing I've ever heard.

The warm welcome I received from my mates' family turned me into a puddle of goo on the inside. "Well," I said, inhaling my sniffle, "I brought pies and beer, but can conjure up anything else you want. Just say the word."

"Oh, no, I couldn't ask you to do such a thing. We're okay, I think," Nancy said with a smile.

Tabby, on the other hand, clapped her hands together in glee. "What can you do?"

I slid onto the seat beside her. "Pretty much anything."

"Oh! Well, how about lemon meringue pie?" she asked before she dropped her voice to a whisper. "But maybe hide the whole magic thing if you can? A lot of these wolves can be bigots, unfortunately."

I swung my legs around and held my hands under the table, magicking up a pie with a perfect meringue top a mile high. When I brought my hands back out, I placed the pie on the table and grinned. "Here's one I prepared earlier," I said cheerily like they did on bad daytime cooking show on TV.

Tabby cackled with laughter, her delight palpable. "Oh my God, that's so cool!"

"Here you are!" Damon's deep voice came from behind me.

I jumped up to greet them, my whole world lighting up even brighter.

"We thought you might have gotten lost," he said.

They didn't kiss me or reach for me, but Chase's hand twitched at his sides when he came up behind Damon. "Did you get in okay?" he asked.

"Yeah... fine," I said vaguely, not wanting to make an issue of it.

Bill scoffed. "Not quite. That idiot, Matthew, grabbed her when she tried to walk through the pack. You might want to arrive together if you're going to invite Jaydy to these things, just to be safe. You know how old hostilities and tempers flare."

Damon's face went dark. "He grabbed you?"

"It was just..." I tried to explain that it was okay, that it was no big deal—prejudice was something I was certainly familiar with— but Damon was already gone.

Chase began to back away too, with furtive glances over his shoulder. "Ah... this isn't going to be pretty, so I better go too."

"Why? What's going on?" Tabby called out after Chase.

"Um... well, we were going to announce this in a much nicer way, but since Damon's taken things upon himself to—"

There was a loud outcry in the direction of Matthew's family group.

Chase called out, "Jaydy's our mate! We wanted you guys to be the first to know. But... well, I better..." Chase ran.

Tabby came at me like a tornado again, squealing and wrapping her arms around me. "Really? Oh my God, that's so awesome!"

I laughed and hugged her in return. "Yeah... I'm not sure if they were in their right minds when they made that decision. Your brothers could do *so* much better than me," I said, falling into my old, self-deprecating ways.

"Oh, nonsense! Don't be ridiculous," Tabby said, pulling back as she pretended to whack me. "You're awesome! The best, honestly, and I won't hear another word about it."

I couldn't help but smile at her. I was wonderful in some ways, but not the obvious ones. Which meant I could only hope that everyone could see past the outer shell to the woman I was underneath it all.

Bill walked over and smiled at me before scratching his neck. "I better go mediate the impending shit show, but welcome to the family, Jaydy." Then Bill wandered off to find the fight—a fight over my honor.

My honor... would wonders never cease?

I sat on the park bench and chuckled to myself. When did that happen? When had I found two men willing to fight for me, and a soon-to-be father-in-law who would back them up without hesitation?

"Welcome to the family!" Nancy reiterated, handing me a glass of white wine.

"Thanks," I smiled back, relieved our revelation had gone over so well. "I know with me being witch it's a bit strange but..."

Nancy shook her head. "Not anymore, it's not. Tania broke the mold, and it's high time this pack changed its views. And if they don't want to, I'm afraid my sons and husband are going to make them."

I laughed and hugged my future mother-in-law. Life was changing, that was for sure, and I was *more* than grateful for her supportive nature. "Did you want some help with any of the food?" I asked as we returned to our table.

About half an hour later, the men returned to the table, sporting a few extra bruises and a cut lip, but otherwise looking fine.

"Are you guys okay?" I asked, momentarily deflated to see them injured at all.

This time Chase came right up to me and put his arms around my waist and kissed me on the lips. "Better now."

A breathless moment later Damon tugged me out of Chase's arms and hugged me tightly. "I'm too bloody to kiss you, but wish I could," he lamented.

I smiled with a wink and ran my fingertips lightly over his face, healing the small bumps and cuts as if they'd never been there at all. "Is this where you say, 'You should see the other guy'?"

Damon chuckled, then kissed me hard, stealing my breath away.

"You *should* see the other guys," Bill said, rubbing his knuckles. "The idiots tried to fight us even after Damon and Chase proclaimed you were their Fated mate."

"They didn't!" Nancy said, looking shocked. "Even after Tania? Unbelievable."

Bill groaned as he sat at the table. "Yep. So, long story short, they deserved their ass kicking."

I couldn't help but grin and lean into the embrace of my men. I'd never felt so loved or protected, and it was a dizzying feeling. "You know I could have kicked his ass with my magic?" I whispered up to Damon.

He nodded. "Yeah, I do. But there's something *so* much more satisfying about punching a guy right in his smug face."

I laughed, feeling giddy. How could I not?

I have a family again...

Nancy pulled the covers off the food with an exuberant smile. "Well, what are you waiting for?" she asked brightly. "Dig in!"

And so, we did. The rest of our night was filled with laughter, family stories, and random conversation. And the guys didn't leave me alone for the rest of the night. Damon or Chase had a hand on me at *all* times. I felt so loved that it made my entire body bubble with joy. It seemed like a lifetime since I'd had this.

And when it finally came time to leave, the whole family walked me back to my car, and I drove home, my spirits soaring.

Life is finally looking up!

CHAPTER 19

JAYDY

The next few days passed in an absolute blur. I went to work and taught my potions students, trained harder than ever at the gym, then spent the nights in my lovers' arms. It was all too good to be true, and I couldn't help but feel the other shoe was about to drop. I'd never felt so good, content, or beautiful in my life.

Unfortunately, after my ex, Steve, had left me, I'd fallen into a negative thinking trap, believing that if something could go wrong, it would.

I tried to shake the feeling, but there felt like there was *something* just beyond the horizon, waiting to ruin everything for me. And then on Friday, the day before the competition, I received a strange voice-mail. I was on my lunch break at work when I took a moment to listen to the message from a caller at an unknown number.

"Jaydy, I need your help. Can you meet me at our favorite restau-rant for dinner tonight?"

My heart sank when I heard his voice. It was Steve, my ex.

What the fuck?

It had been so long since he'd called me, and even though I'd spent a long time hoping for this very moment, now that it had arrived, my heart rebelled. I thought I'd made my position perfectly clear to him the last time we'd accidentally run into each other. I didn't want to talk to him, and I certainly didn't want to meet him for dinner.

Not now that I have a new life and mates! Plural!

He didn't need me. He'd certainly made that abundantly clear, which made this phone call seem even more odd. My guts roiled, and I pursed my lips in thought. There was no way we were getting mixed signals, so there was only one reason he'd conceivably contact me, and that made me feel even more uneasy and put on the spot.

He must really be in trouble if he's messaging me for help. Ugh.

Out of everyone he could have contacted, he'd chosen me. Steve was a powerful warlock in his own right, as was everyone in his entire family, even his new girlfriend.

Maybe something is wrong with her?

I decided to do the right thing, following my head instead of my heart, and texted him straight away.

I can call you after work. What's wrong?

He didn't get back to me until hours later.

No. I need to see you in person. Can we meet at 7pm?

No! Hell, no! Was my initial reaction, but that was coming from a place of fear and rejection, and I needed to think about this rationally, not emotionally. I pressed my lips together into a thin line, thinking about the repercussions of such a dinner. I'd told my guys I needed a quiet night at home before the competition tomorrow, so *technically* I was free. But they wouldn't like it, I was sure.

My inner urge to help, heal, and protect bubbled at the fringes of my consciousness. I'd always put myself out for others, that's who I was. I counted empathy and kindness among my most favored and valued personal virtues. I couldn't very well ignore Steve simply because he was *the ex*. That was immature, and I was better than that.

And what if Steve actually does need my help? What if this is genuine? Fuck it.

Come hell or high water, I needed to know, or it would eat at me until I couldn't sleep. I'd tell my mates later and they'd understand—they loved me for who I was. All the same, a small, defensive, and fickle inner voice warned me that I may get burned. But I had to *at least* find out what was wrong, or I'd never forgive myself if something serious happened. Still grimacing, I texted him back, my stomach twisting as I did.

Fine. But I can't stay long.

Thank you. See you soon!

I sighed heavily, already anxious and partially regretting my decision.

But it's the right thing to do.

I'd remind myself of the fact over and over if necessary. I was no slave to my emotions. Glancing at the time on my phone, I realized it was just before 4 pm. If I pushed hard to make gains, I could fit in a training session, shower and change, and still get to the Japanese restaurant Steve was talking about in good time. It had never been my favorite, but it was his. And I knew how his mind worked.

Unfortunately.

I went to the gym, hoping to see my gorgeous guys, but they weren't there. The immediate disappointment I felt was rather shocking, but I wasn't going to let that get the better of me, so I changed and got to work. I trained for two solid hours, keeping one eye on the door the whole time.

When I'd finally finished, I was still ridiculously wishing they'd walk in through the door and tell me it was okay to go and meet Steve, to find out what he needed. I shouldn't have allowed myself to be so disappointed when they didn't appear, especially since I was the one that told them not to come in the first place. They'd respected my wishes, understanding I needed some down time before the competition which was great... mostly.

George sauntered up to me with a grin. "I heard through the grapevine that you finally let the wolf shifters woo you, Jaydy."

I grinned as I wiped my face with a sweat towel. "Well, you know… they were pretty persistent."

George grinned at me in return. "Yeah, I can see that." He glanced around. "But they're not here cheering you on before the big comp?"

I took a sip of water from my bottle and zipped up my gym bag. "They'll be there tomorrow," I said. "I was just trying to get an early night tonight, that's all. I could use the rest."

He crossed his beefy arms over his chest with a knowing wink. "Yeah, I can't imagine they'd let you go to sleep early."

Taking that as my cue, I gave him a playful shove and a smile before bustling past him. "Bye bye, George!" I called back, throwing my bag over my shoulder before heading out of the gym and walking to my car.

There were texts on my phone waiting for me from both Chase and Damon, telling me how much they missed me, and that they'd see me bright and early tomorrow. The messages made me smile, and I sent them texts straight back. I'd call them tonight after I'd spoken to Steve and found out what he wanted. My best guess was that he'd heard about the "big-girl magic" and wanted my help with a spell, or potion, or something.

Nothing else makes any sense.

Once home, I showered and changed into something suitable for the Japanese restaurant Steve liked so much. I was careful to choose something that wasn't feminine or revealed any cleavage. Not because Steve would like it better that way, but so that he wouldn't be misled into thinking I was trying to dress up for him. It was quite the opposite, in fact. I was making every effort to dress down.

When I arrived at the restaurant, my anxiety grew notch by notch, until I couldn't shake the strange niggling feeling that'd wormed its way into the pit of my stomach.

This feels wrong.

"Jaydy!" Steve's voice came from behind me.

I jumped and turned around in response, uneasy and taken by surprise.

He wrapped me up in a very familiar hug that made my skin crawl.

"Oh... hello," I said, patting him on the back and pulling away quickly.

He had a big smile on his face, the type that in the past would have had me falling all over myself. Tonight, however, it sent chills down my spine.

"Hey, Steve... I was just thinking..."

He put his hand in the small of my back and ushered me into the restaurant. "Thank you so much for coming. I made a reservation for us." He turned to the maître d'. "Reservation under Daniels."

The man looked at his book. "Right this way."

With a sinking feeling, I let him guide me to my seat in the middle of the quiet restaurant.

"Wine list?" The maître d' asked.

I shook my head. "No, thank you. I won't be staying long."

Steve frowned at me. "What are you talking about? We're here for dinner."

I sighed, feeling like I was right back to where I was about a year ago. Fighting with him for any sense of self-worth and autonomy. "Steve, I have a competition tomorrow, plus... I'm seeing someone, and they're waiting for my call."

Steve's face turned thunderous before he cleared the look and smiled again, a literal Jekyll and Hyde right before my eyes. He turned to the man and nodded. "The most expensive bottle of red wine you have, thank you."

Damn it. Why does he have to be such a jerk?

He waved the man away with a condescending flick of his hand, then he fixed his gaze on me again. "I didn't realize you were dating again."

I stared at him, trying not to let my face do the speaking for me. "Um... again? We broke up more than a year ago, Steve. So, yeah, of course, I'm dating again. I've moved on. You'd moved on before we even broke up."

"Oh, you don't know?" he said softly, his face full of mock surprise. "I broke up with Tessie weeks ago."

"Weeks ago, huh?" I repeated. "No, I didn't know that."

No one said anything to me. Not George at the gym, nor anyone at work. Not that I made it a habit to ask about Steve, but I would have thought that if there was gossip to hear, I would have heard it.

A long, uncomfortable silence passed between us before he reached over the table and took my hand in his.

My jaw dropped and my heart pounded in my chest. "What are you—"

"I love you Jaydy," he said, his tone filled with what sounded like genuine longing. "I never stopped."

I scoffed at him. "You... what?"

How dare he?

"I made the biggest mistake of my life when I left you..." His voice trailed off as he squeezed my hand. "You are the woman I'm meant to be with. That's why I broke up with Tessie."

Her name on his lips made me want to vomit, and I pulled my hand out of his grasp in no small amount of revulsion. "Well... I'm sorry to hear that, Steve," I said carefully. "But I'm not available."

Not anymore and especially not to you. Ever!

The head waiter arrived with the wine my ex requested, bringing the awkward moment to a standstill.

Steve approved the bottle with a flippant wave of his hand,

The waiter served us both, filling our glasses.

I didn't bother trying to stop him. I was going to need some liquid courage if this conversation continued any further. A small amount of alcohol would steel my nerves and give me the resolve I needed.

Steve lifted his wine to toast in a celebratory way. "What shall we drink to?" he asked, his brow crooked.

I picked up my glass and held it high with a wry smile. "How about to my win tomorrow? I'm competing in a new event for the first time."

As expected, he hated my idea. His rule when we'd been together was that all toasts had to be about *everyone*, and preferably something from which he could benefit. His lips thinned as his smile dropped, but he clinked my glass. "Yes, Jaydy. Here's to your success."

I took a small sip of wine, then another. My stomach was empty, and I was beginning to wish I'd eaten more post workout. But I didn't want to stay and eat with Steve, even if I was hungry.

"So, tell me about the guy you're seeing," Steve invited, swirling the wine in his glass nonchalantly. "Assuming it is a man, of course."

I gave him a forced smile. "Yes, his name is Damon." I wasn't sure why I chose Damon's name over Chase's, but it was the first thing that came to my lips, and I certainly wasn't going to admit to dating two men at once. It was unusual by most people's standards, *and* it was none of his business.

"Well, I hope he makes you happy, Jaydy. You certainly deserve it."

"Hmm," I agreed, nodding as I sipped more of the wine. It warmed my empty belly, comforting me, but it also made me want to tell him things, which was strange, to say the least. I didn't truly trust Steve as far as I could throw him. I licked my lips, my brow furrowing as I resisted the feeling.

Talk about booze going to your head!

"Tell me more," he said, his tone oddly cajoling.

I opened my mouth to answer him truthfully, then caught myself. My ex-boyfriend, the one who'd taken advantage of me, stayed in my home rent-free, and dumped me for a woman half my size, didn't deserve any of the details about my life. "No... it's all good," I said, slurring a little, my heart racing as my mind seemed to slow. "Tell me why you asked me to meet you here. I thought you might want some help with a... with a..."

Shit. What's the word?

I was struggling to concentrate. "Spell," I finished.

Yes! That was the word.

He snorted a little in laughter.

"What?" I demanded, lifting my chin in annoyance as I fought the drowsiness that was attempting to overcome me.

Wow, I must have pushed myself way too hard at the gym.

I shouldn't have had any damn alcohol.

He smiled at me and this time I saw fragments of the old, smug Steve. The one that greeted me with sharp words and cruelty every time I made a mistake or didn't live up to his expectations. "Just... you." He gestured to me in an obnoxious way. "It's really true, isn't it? That you have a lot of new power because you're... well... *overweight*."

I glared at him, my cheeks flushing with heat. "I am not overweight! I'm a powerlifter. I'm strong *and* fit. You have no right to speak to me like that," I stammered as I shook my head. My vision was drifting in and out of focus now.

What is going on?

Steve didn't sound like he was struggling to speak though. He sounded, well, happy, if anything.

I pushed myself to my feet, struggling under the weight of whatever that asshole had obviously put in my wine.

Fucking classic, abusive Steve. I should have known!

I felt so angry at myself. For once, I should have trusted the jaded voice in my head. Not everyone needed my help—or could be helped.

Me and my stupid rose-colored glasses...

I hated that kindness could be used as a weapon against you, that it could be seen as a weakness. "I've got to go."

"No."

"Yes!" I stumbled toward the exit. I still hadn't mastered the spell that would have allowed me to magically teleport from one place to another, and in this state, I didn't have enough control to try that sort of magic anyway. I had to get out of the restaurant before—

"Come with me, Jaydy," Steve said, grabbing my elbow and helping me out of the restaurant.

Once outside, I inhaled deeply, assuming the cool, clear air would help me feel better. Maybe I'd been wrong about Steve drugging me and I was just seriously dehydrated and fatigued from the workout? But I wasn't wrong. The more my heart raced and the more I sucked in great lungfuls of fresh air, the cloudier my thoughts and vision became. "What did you... do..." I accused Steve, staggering away from him.

He let me go but walked behind me like a stalker.

In desperation, I used the restaurant's wall as a guide. I could barely see now at all.

Fucking hell!

I needed to call out for help, but my throat was constricted, and it was becoming harder to remain upright.

I need my men. Oh, God... they don't even know where I am! How are they going to find me?

"This way, Jaydy," Steve cajoled, grabbing my elbow and tugging me away from the wall.

"No!" I tried to scream, but my attempt came out as a mere whisper.

"No need to fight," he said gently, darkly. "That wine had a powerful spell in every sip. You won't be able to see soon, nor speak. But don't worry, it's only temporary."

"Why?" I managed to gasp.

He shoved me into a car seat, or that was what it felt like from the chair beneath me and the smells around me.

I was panicking so hard I thought my head would explode, but my heart didn't race anymore. It couldn't. It thudded along dully as no adrenaline failed to course through me. All the worry was trapped with me inside my own mind as my body became paralyzed.

Steve shut the door, then as my vision completely disappeared, I heard another door open and him getting in.

Holy fuck. He's actually abducting me!

"Why!" I hissed again, forcing myself to keep breathing. He obviously wanted me alive, but why? My mind raged and swirled with emotion.

Why is he doing this?

"I need your power," he said, as though it was the simplest answer in the world. "I know you wouldn't just give it to me, so..."

"I would have helped you," I managed to wheeze out, my eyelids falling shut as my head fell back against the headrest.

He scoffed at me and roughly pulled the seatbelt over me from the driver's seat.

I cringed at his touch but couldn't move to stop him. Tears leaked from my eyes as the weight of my helplessness washed over me. What was he going to do with me?

"I don't want your help," he spat at me. "I want your power. And there's only one way to get it," he said, his words left hanging threateningly in the air between us. He started the car and pulled out onto the street.

My only hope was that my wolf shifters would come looking for me. But how could they? They didn't even know I'd met up with Steve for dinner, and they wouldn't think to check on me. Not tonight. I'd specifically told them not to so that I could rest.

Oh God! Fuck.

My last thoughts of hope went up in a puff of smoke as my strength gave out, and I fell into a deep and bottomless darkness. I'd just made the biggest damn mistake of my life...

CHAPTER 20

DAMON

Tania had offered to host the powerlifting competition at her gym, since she had all the equipment, and half the state's competitors already trained there. The woman was smart and more than a little business savvy, I'd give her that.

When we arrived at the gym, the place was completely transformed. Most of the equipment had been removed, and there were multiple stations set up, even a dais for the champions in the corner to receive their awards. They'd also shifted the front desks and partitioning walls to open the space up even further.

"This looks great," Chase said, grinning as he looked around at everyone.

There were a lot of people signing up, but we walked through to the main area, in search of Jaydy.

I glanced down at my cell phone again, anxiety biting into me.

Nothing.

"Have you heard from Jaydy?" I asked my brother, just in case he had.

Chase frowned, taking his cell out of his pocket, then shook his head. "No. Why? Are you worried?"

"Yeah... I am." I'd woken up this morning with a deep sense of unease in my gut. I'd put it down to sleeping away from my mate for the first time since we'd sorted everything out and gotten together properly. It had been impossible to believe, but I'd been lonely and cold last night for the first time.

I'd never known how great it could feel to sleep next to someone until I'd held Jaydy's body against mine through the night. Now that I'd experienced that feeling of perfection, I didn't want to go back to being alone. I just couldn't imagine it. I didn't want to even try.

"Me too," Chase said with a hefty sigh. "I didn't want to say anything, but... yeah, it feels wrong. Do you feel it too?"

I stared at my brother, then realized we were being idiots. We were trying to be normal boyfriends, whatever that really meant. But the obvious truth was that we shouldn't be ignoring our instincts. We were purebred wolf shifters of ten generations. If something felt wrong, then it usually was. "We need to find her. She should be here already. Something's not right."

Chase nodded, putting his cell phone to his ear. "I'll try calling her now."

I nodded. "I'll go find Tania."

Chase grabbed me before I headed off in search of Jaydy's best friend. "Actually, I might head over to her house, just in case she's slept in or something."

I didn't get the chance to reply.

Chase just took off running, his phone to his ear all the while. Jaydy's place was only about five minutes away, so it was a good plan. In five to seven minutes, we'd either know if she was okay... or that she wasn't.

We have to do something.

My intuition said something was amiss. I'd be *so* happy to be proven wrong, but my gut told me that wasn't going to happen. I did another quick scan of the room, even though I knew Jaydy wasn't there. Then I spotted Leo and hurried over to him.

"Hey, Damon," Leo said, giving me a bro style hug. "I heard you and Jaydy—"

I stopped him mid-sentence. "Yeah, we are... but we can't find her."

Leo frowned at me. "What do you mean, you can't find her?" Before I could answer, Leo called out and waved his hand. "Tania!"

Tania came running over. "What's up? I have a million things to do still."

Leo crossed his arms over his chest. "Tell her," he encouraged me.

I turned toward the glowing bride. She was tanned and smiling and had lost a little weight. Probably because Leo and Mason had kept her busy in bed all day. "We can't find Jaydy."

Tania narrowed her eyes at me. "What do you mean?"

"I mean, we don't know where she is. Last night she told us she wanted the night off from sleeping together to get to bed early, you know, because of the competition." I waved my hand around to indicate the gym.

Tania took out her phone and hit a button, then put her cell to her ear. "When did you last hear from her?"

"About five o'clock last night," I said. "But she told us not to check in. She said she needed to focus." I'd been a little hurt at the time, but I kind of understood. We *did* text her a lot.

Tania put the phone down again. "It's going straight to her voicemail, so either her phone's dead or—"

"Or what?" A shiver of unease moved over me, my heartrate increasing with each breath. "What is it? Tell me."

Tania began to fidget. "Jaydy would never miss a competition. So, she could still be asleep with her phone off... maybe."

It was only nine o'clock, so although it was possible, it wasn't likely. That girl got herself up at 7am every morning even without an alarm. "Well, Chase has driven over to her house, so we'll find out soon enough." Just as I said the words, my cell rang. "Did you find her?" I asked. Meg's distressed meowing came through loud and clear on the phone. "Chase?"

"She's not here, and from the looks of Meg, she didn't come home last night either."

I could hear Chase soothing the cat and pouring dry food into her dish.

"Why do you think that?" I asked, my heart beginning to pound sickeningly hard against my ribs.

"Meg has no water or no food, and from the looks and smell of her bedroom, Jaydy didn't sleep here last night. Her scent is old, not like she was just here recently."

"Holy shit. Okay. Come back. I'm with Tania. We'll come up with a plan."

"Okay. I'll be right back," Chase said as he hung up.

I turned to Tania. "Chase says there's no sign of her, and she didn't sleep at home last night. Meg was left with no food or water, so unless she's got some amazing boyfriend we don't know about..."

Tania scoffed. "She'd never leave Meg without setting up someone to feed her."

"Then where could she be?" Leo asked. "Does she have any enemies? Could she have been in a car accident?"

George sauntered up to us. "Hey, guys, what's going on?"

We caught him up on the situation.

The big guy's eyebrows drew down, getting more and more angry. "What the hell... Hang on. I thought I saw her car. It was parked outside that Japanese restaurant on the north side. I dismissed the thought because it didn't make sense why she'd be out the night before a comp, but now I think about it, it was her car. Same little red Beetle with cat stickers on the back window."

My heart sank. "What the... Why would she go out last night? She said—"

Tania's face paled and she swallowed hard. "Steve..."

I frowned. "Is that the ex asshole?"

She nodded. "They went to that restaurant *all* the time when they were together. Do you think he might have lured her out to meet him?"

"And what?" I demanded, crossing my arms over my racing heart as my wolf rose within me. "What are you suggesting?" After all we'd shared, could Jaydy really be cheating on us? Would she have run back to the boyfriend who'd treated her so badly? It hurt to even think she'd do such a thing, but was it possible?

"Fuck," George groaned. "I heard rumors, but... *Fuck!*"

"What did you hear?" Tania asked.

George slammed his hand into his forehead, then tugged at his hair in frustration. "Listen, I haven't said anything to you because I didn't want to upset you. It's not your fault, so it's bullshit."

"Get to the point!" Tania said, waving her hand as if to say, "Don't worry about that shit."

"Okay, well, there are *a lot* of witches, and warlocks too, who are pretty cut up about the new power that the big girls have now. Thanks to you, Tania, Harry, and the genie spell."

Tania groaned. "No... that wasn't my intention."

I grabbed George's arm harder than I should have. "I'm not getting it. What are you saying? That Jaydy caught up with her ex-boyfriend because he wanted her to do a spell for him or something?"

That kind of made sense. Maybe he needed her power to boost a spell of his, the same way Jaydy had called in the Ancient to be her back up. That wasn't cheating, although why wouldn't she just tell us she was meeting up with him? We wouldn't have liked it, sure, but we wouldn't have stopped her.

George was silent and glanced at Tania.

I squeezed his thick forearm, then shook it a little. "Don't play games with me, George. Tell me. Is she cheating on us, or—"

"Oh, God no!" George said, shaking his head. "I'm afraid that Steve or his girlfriend would be willing to strip Jaydy of her newfound power, given the opportunity... and she's ripped at the moment. She's been training hard, and her magic would be at full potential right now."

Chase came running back into the gym. "So, what do we know?"

I turned to him. "Jaydy's car is parked outside a Japanese restaurant in the Witch side of town she used to frequent with her ex. George and Tania think Steve may have lured her there to steal her new powers or something."

Tania was looking more and more worried. There were tears in her eyes now.

I turned toward her. "When you say that they could strip her power, do you mean she'd be okay, but human afterward?" We could handle a human mate as long as we had Jaydy, safe and sound. It didn't matter to us what magic she did or didn't have.

Tania shook her head sadly. "No, if we're right, and I think George is onto something, here. That fuckhead Steve is a *true* narcissist. He wouldn't think twice about stealing Jaydy's magic if it made him more powerful."

I wanted to shake Tania in my frustration.

Why isn't anyone giving me a straight answer?

Leo hurried forward then stuck close to her, ready to intercept if I tried to so much as touch his mate.

I could see it in the way he moved. I pressed my hand to my temple. "Spit it out. *Please.* Just make it make sense. What does it mean?"

Tania bit her lip, then glanced over at George before answering. "It means Jaydy could die."

Chase gasped beside me. "No!"

My eyes shifted, and I saw red, or in this case, black and white, as my wolf ripped through me.

Chase began pushing Tania out of my way. "Step back, guys, he's lost control."

And I had. I had no way of stopping the shift as a growl tore through my vocal cords and I dropped to all fours.

There were shouts of surprise as Chase and George managed the crowd.

My wolf body shredded my clothes apart, and I used every shred of my control to force myself to stay in one place, to not run or move, to make sure I didn't hurt anyone.

Well, almost anyone. Wherever that fucker Steve, is, he's dead!

CHAPTER 21

JAYDY

Fading in and out of consciousness was torture in the worst possible way. I had absolutely no control over my own body, nor my own will. I'd wake up just long enough to blink my eyes open to see the two people in the world I hated the most—Steve and his pathetic bitch of a side piece. Then, before I had the mind to formulate anything to say, I'd pass out again. But when I finally gathered the strength to remain awake for more than a few minutes, I managed to hear them talking.

"You gave her too much," Tessie hissed at him in annoyance. "She's *still* not awake."

"So?" Steve said, sounding bored. "Just drain her now."

"I can't!" Tessie said and made a thumping sound. Did she stomp her foot or punch Steve?

I hope she punched Steve. Fucking asshole.

"Why not?" he asked.

"Her magic is linked to her strength! She has to be awake. It won't work otherwise. That's why I told you to wait until after the competition on Saturday in the first place and not before. You should never have grabbed her last night."

Fucking bitch. She's smart, though. I'm going to have to watch out for her.

Their arguing voices faded again, and I fell into the void of my spell-induced coma once more. Sometime later, the final time I woke up, I was being manhandled, pulled up, and moved onto a table. I couldn't fight them, but I certainly wasn't going to help them. I stayed as non-compliant and floppy as possible.

"Wakey, wakey," Steve said, slapping my cheeks.

I instinctively frowned, even though I tried not to respond.

"I know you're awake Jaydy," my ex said. "Open your eyes, or I'll fucking sticky tape them open."

Begrudgingly and very slowly, I struggled to open my eyes, blinking at the bright light streaming in the windows. It was day now and hopefully later than it felt. Surely, Damon and Chase would have realized I was missing by now, and they'd be trying to find me. I looked around to try and ascertain where I was. I was lying on my back, on a table, in what looked like a living room. But it wasn't one I'd seen before.

Perhaps this is Tessie's house? She lives on the north side... but where?

"Is she awake? Oh, goody!" The plastic, blonde, Barbie doll was clapping her hands in glee at my pain.

I lifted my head and glared at her. "What the hell are you two doing with me?"

"We're going to take *all* your new power," she said with a gratuitous smile. "You don't need it."

Steve conjured up ropes and tied my arms and legs down to the table.

I tried to struggle, to lift my hands and tear at the bonds, but I was still too weak and groggy. With no other option available to me, I tried another tact. "You'll never get any of my magic now. I can't even move, thanks to whatever the hell that spell was in my drink last night."

Tessie pouted her pink-stained lips. "Oh, yes... Stevey got a bit overzealous and doubled the dose I gave him. Silly man. But not to worry! We'll give it another couple of hours, and you should be back to full strength, so to speak."

"So to speak?" I growled at her, wrenching at the bindings that held down my arms.

"Well, yes," she said, taunting me as she reached out to touch my leg, running her long, painted nails over my thick thigh.

I flinched and glared harder at her. "Don't touch me! Fuck off."

She laughed, and her high-pitched chuckle sounded almost insane. "How did Steve ever take a woman like you to his bed? You're just so fat and ugly."

"Ask him," I said flicking my gaze toward Steve. "We were together three years and were living together the *whole* time," I emphasized. "And he had no problem with my body then," I taunted right back.

He had, of course. He definitely had. It was the main reason he broke up with me. He'd been critical of me every damn day, but I wasn't going to tell his crazy girlfriend that. Anything I could say to ruffle her pristine feathers was worth saying.

Her smile faltered, and she looked toward Steve. "Is that true?"

"Of course, not," he said, grabbing her hand. "She was always ugly to me. You know that."

I forced a laugh from my throat, although I knew what he was saying was actually the truth. He'd put up with me, hoping I'd change into what he wanted. But now wasn't the time to share that. I had to buy myself more time. "Three years? You fucked me for three *years* and hated it every single time, did you? Tell her another lie, why don't you?"

"Shut up, bitch!" Steve snarled, leaning over to slap me.

I bit my lip in an effort not to cry out as abrupt, stinging pain flashed across my face.

Fucking asshole. You're losing it!

My face heated with shame and anger, but I forced another smile to my lips, feeling my magic gathering within me to fight back.

"Okay, Steve. Whatever you have to tell yourself so that you can sleep at night."

Tessie flicked her long blonde hair over her shoulder as she turned around and stormed out of the room, ever the drama queen.

Steve ran after her.

I relaxed against the table, reaching for my magic. It was there, and it was thankfully growing. I tried to release the ropes on the table that held me down, but my magic couldn't budge them—not yet, at least.

"Gah..." God only knew what sort of magic spell Steve had put in my wine last night, courtesy of Tessie. Whatever the spell was, it had knocked me out, but it also made it feel like my power was on the back burner or something. They'd fucked me over, but they'd royally screwed themselves as well in the process if they were planning to take all my magic. It wasn't there for the taking, and who knows how long it would take to return. Tessie had said a few hours, but how could they know?

I have to find a way out of here.

They weren't going to simply take my power and then hand me back to my mates as a non-magical. That would be bad enough, of course. I'd lose my job and my ability to help anyone. I'd be stripped of something that inherently made me who I was. But that wasn't their intention.

Magic-stripping was highly illegal, and they'd be severely punished if they were ever found out. Which they would be, given that I worked at the Magic School.

Which means there's only one outcome to this. They are going to kill me!

Whether they'd do it directly or via the spell that would strip my magic, I couldn't know. But once they were done with me, they'd get rid of the evidence, and I'd become just another Missing Person report on the daily news.

I must stop them.

I started to calculate the hours I had ahead of me before my power returned to full strength, because that's precisely what they were waiting for.

I need a plan. Think, Jaydy, think!

I wracked my brain, fighting the part of me that was straight up panicking. I was apparently destined to die today, so I had to focus on coming up with a plan that would help me survive. My mates would come for me soon. I had to believe that. But just in case they didn't find me in time, I had to find a way to save myself.

Focus. Breathe. Focus.

I closed my eyes, took a slow, calming breath, then started looking around again. The bright daylight coming in the windows meant it was already Saturday morning. The event would have started, and I would be missed. That fact worked in my favor.

Maybe I can send a message to Tania or George?

I closed my eyes and visualized writing a note and sending it on magical wings to Tania. I got halfway through the spell and my magic failed. It was almost like someone had pulled the plug on the TV. The spell just simply fizzled out. "Fuck," I muttered in frustration under my breath.

Steve must have put something extra in the wine last night to render my magic useless while it was recharging within me!

That, or Tessie had put wards up around her house so that my spells couldn't penetrate to the world beyond. That was definitely a possibility. That witch was more powerful than most, and it was one of the many reasons Steve had wanted her.

Power-hungry asshole!

Either way, I needed to find a way to get a message to Tania or one of the guys. Anyone at all who could help... because tied to the table as I was *and* magicless left me severely fucked.

And it was the worst sort of irony that the moment my life had *finally* started heading in the right direction, that a beautiful, young, skinny, and powerful witch came in to snatch everything from me. They were stealing more than my power, they were stealing my life, my happiness.

I closed my eyes and swallowed the jagged lump in my throat. This was definitely *bad*, but I couldn't give up. Damon and Chase would never forgive me if I did.

Oh, God...

All the blood drained from my face as a secondary thought occurred to me, wiggling to the forefront of my mind. In my research, I'd read about what happened to Fated mates if their woman died. This wasn't just about me anymore.

Fuck! My men won't survive if I don't.

My heart filled with equal amounts of despair and rage at the idea of their beautiful hearts no longer beating. Our lives were now intrinsically linked forever.

No... they can't die. I won't let that happen!

I opened my eyes and stared up at the bullshit pink ceiling, allowing the strength of my emotions to continue to build and bolster me. I had to get out of there. I had to survive.

With or without my magic, I must get out of here alive. If not for myself, then for my mates!

Their lives were literally now in my hands, and I would *not* be the reason they were no longer a part of this world.

CHAPTER 22

CHASE

He won't hurt anyone!" I called out reassuringly, stepping toward my brother, who had completely lost control and shifted into his wolf. "He's just upset. Our mate has been kidnapped."

The room full of humans, witches, and warlocks came closer, encircling us.

Shit... humans!

"Tania!" I called out to the owner of the gym. "The humans?"

"Fuck," Her eyes widened in instant understanding, and she nodded. A heartbeat later, she began to chant, and one by one, the humans in the room began to sink to the floor as Tania's magic took effect.

"Catch them!" I called out to the others, rushing forward to help a woman who was now fast asleep.

"And lock the doors!" Mason called out to the guys at the back.

The room was chaotic for several breathless moments, but soon enough, only the shifters and magic folk were still standing, and everyone else was sound asleep and oblivious as to what was going on.

"Listen up!" Tania called out, clapping her hands for everyone's attention. "Jaydy's missing, and we believe she's been taken by Steve and his new girlfriend. Does anyone know where they live now?"

Daniella gasped and rushed forward. "Are you serious?"

I nodded and heaved a heavy sigh. "We are. Do you know where they live?"

Dani pointed to a guy in a bright orange tank top. "Hopper, you know where Tessie lives, don't you?"

The guy nodded but frowned. "I don't think they'd take Jaydy. Why would they?"

"That's not the point," Dani snapped at him before I could get a word out. "You trust Tania, don't you? Well?"

The guy nodded with an acquiescing grimace.

Tania took a step toward the warlock. "Then tell us where they live, and if Jaydy's not there, then we need to find her. She's missing and could be in trouble."

I glanced around at the room full of witches and warlocks. "Could you all do a spell to locate her? Is that possible?"

Damon walked over to me and pressed into my leg. He hadn't been able to shift back just yet, but he wasn't running, which was a good sign. He'd be able to return to human form soon enough.

Tania looked around the room hopefully, waiting for someone to offer their assistance.

Dani walked over to us, standing off to the side of Damon, making her choice.

I understood the move for what it was, and a small wave of gratitude washed over me.

"Why should we help a wolf shifter?" some big guy called out.

Tania immediately pointed at the door. "Tim, get out!" she demanded. "And anyone else that feels that way can fuck right off. You're no longer welcome here."

Tim grabbed his bag and left, as did a couple of other people. But everyone who stayed surged closer.

"I want to help," said a girl with pink-tipped hair.

"Me, too," Dani said, crossing her arms over her chest in case it wasn't obvious to everyone. "If Jaydy's in trouble, we *have* to help her. She's our friend!"

Hopper slid around a group of women to step forward. "All right, I know where Tessie and Steve live. I can give you the address."

"Thank you. We'll go now," I said, pulling out my phone. "Can you type it in here?"

"We'll stay and see what we can do on the magic front," Tania offered. "My guys will keep in contact too."

Leo nodded. "Do you guys want back-up?"

I shook my head. "No, thanks. We've got this."

"No, you don't," George said sternly, grabbing his bag. "I'll go with Chase and Damon. If Steve decides to fight dirty, I've got some magic up my sleeve for him."

I grinned and nodded in appreciation at the huge powerlifter. "We'd appreciate it."

My brother and I certainly had the strength element and raw physical aspect covered, but we could benefit from having a warlock on our side to even out the playing field in the magical department.

Hopper handed back my phone. "Here. It's about fifteen minutes away."

"Let's go," George said.

The crowd parted for us, and we ran for George's vehicle. He had a huge truck to fit his impressive proportions, and it was perfect for a rescue mission.

I jumped up into the passenger side and buckled myself in.

Meanwhile, Damon jumped in the back, still in his wolf form.

"Is he going shift back?" George asked, sliding the key into the ignition and turning the engine over.

I shrugged. "Maybe, but I'm not too worried. He's a lot more powerful this way. Plus, we heal faster in our shifter forms."

George grunted in acknowledgement, and we sped off toward the witch side of the city. He gripped the wheel tightly, taking corners too fast and hard.

My heart began pounding hard in my chest, putting me on edge.

We are going to get Jaydy back.

My phone went off, and it was Leo. I answered immediately. "What's happening?" I asked.

"The witches and warlocks have cast a spell, and Jaydy is definitely in witch side. She's alive, they can tell that much, but they can't get a lock on where she is because the assholes have probably got some kind of wards up or something."

"Thanks, Leo. We're almost there. I'll call you if we need you." I hung up and couldn't help the smile that lifted my lips despite the urgency of the situation. "Hearing Leo talk all warlock is kind of... well, funny."

George spared me a chuckle and a look, then returned to focusing on the road. "What did he say?"

"Basically, Jaydy's alive and she's in definitely in witch side, but they can't get a bead on her because there are wards up or something."

George sighed. "Yeah, I thought that might be the case. Tessie would have wards on her house so no one can hex her in her own home, which probably means we're not going to be able to find Jaydy with a location spell."

There was movement in the backseat, then Damon was back and putting his seat belt on. "Does that mean Jaydy can't use magic inside the wards as well? I mean, if she's alive, why isn't she like trying to magick herself out of there?"

George didn't answer and his lips were pressed into a thin line.

I glanced at Damon, then back at the warlock. "That's bad, yeah?"

George nodded. "Yep. If they wanted to take her magic, then it means they would have probably sedated her. She certainly wouldn't have gone out quietly, I know that much."

"Sedated?" I repeated.

George nodded, and then we fell into an uneasy silence for the rest of the drive. The final corner as were drew near had us slowing down. "We're almost there," the powerlifter announced.

A growl sounded from the backseat and Damon was back into wolf mode.

George pulled the truck up outside number twenty-two. "Her house is that one, over there with the pink front door."

I looked across the road to a house a few numbers up. "It's looks like some kind of damn fairytale cottage." The house was small but had a thatched roof and brightly colored flowers planted out front.

George snorted. "Yeah, you would never know a fucking crazy witch lives there." He unbuckled his seat belt and made to open the door.

I grabbed for his arm, my heart in my throat. "What's the plan here?"

George went ahead and opened the door. "I'm going to go and see if they have Jaydy."

"But…" I breathed.

"Stay here," George said firmly, eyeing us both evenly. "If they see wolf shifters, they'll shoot first and ask questions later. Think of Jaydy and keep your shit together."

Damon growled from the backseat, clearly unimpressed with the request.

"Damn straight," I told him, but I stayed put. Neither of us was willing to endanger our mate any more than she already was. And currently, we had the benefit of the element of surprise.

George jogged over to the house and knocked. Nothing happened, so he started looking in through the windows and knocking on the glass.

Finally, the door opened, and a man answered.

Pure, red-hot hatred filled my gut. "That's the fucking asshole who broke our Jaydy," I snarled. We'd never asked her about her past or her childhood.

Not really. Not in any detail, anyway.

But it was clear that her ex-boyfriend had done a lot of damage to her self-esteem in the time they'd been together. "He doesn't look like much," I observed critically. And he wasn't. He looked weak, too skinny, and he was showing signs of losing his hair.

George shook the guy's hand after a brief conversation, then ambled back to the car.

Jaydy's ex shot George a death glare as he walked away.

I had to dig my fingers into my thighs to stop myself from launching out of the truck and bolting straight in through the front door in response to the arrogance of that prick.

George hopped back into the vehicle, cool as a cucumber, acting as if everything was totally fine and normal.

"Well?" I demanded, my breathing quickening as I waited with bated breath for him to buckle his seatbelt again.

"Oh... she's in there," he answered, wiping sweat from his brow.

"He told you that?" I gaped at him.

George laughed. "Hell no, he's not that stupid. Steve said he saw her for dinner last night, but that she'd headed home early in preparation for the comp this morning. He told me to call him when we found her safe and sound, as if he was concerned about her wellbeing. Fucking prick was lying through his damn teeth."

"How do you know?" I asked, clenching my teeth until I heard them crack in my jaw.

George started the truck again. "I'm going to move around the block so they can't see where we are. They'll assume we've left."

Even though my wolf howled like a rabid beast in my chest, I quieted it down. "You didn't answer me. Tell us how you know she's there."

"I could sense her," he said. "My magic is very intuitive, and I've known Jaydy a *long* time. I couldn't hear her or smell her or anything like that, the way you guys can. I just *know* she's in there."

The anxiety in my chest tightened another notch. "Well, that's good, but we still have to find a way into her, don't we?"

George parked the truck again and sighed. "Yeah, and unfortunately, I felt a huge number of wards on that place. It's thick with them. I'm going to have to use all my magic just to bring down the wards so you can get in and Jaydy can get out."

"Can you do that alone?" I asked. "Or can Tania call the Ancient for help? This seems like it might be up her alley."

"The Ancient?" George repeated, his eyes growing big and wide. "Tania knows an Ancient?"

I nodded, feeling slightly chuffed that I knew something about the magic community that George didn't. "Yeah. Jaydy does too. The Ancient came to our house and helped Jaydy with the spell that fixed my sister's legs."

George pulled out his phone and pushed his speed dial, then activated the speakerphone. The ringing sound echoed around us.

"George! What's happening?" It was Tania.

"Jaydy's definitely inside the house, but they've got wards up the *wazoo* and now that I've tripped the alarm, I bet they're going to hurry up with the spell. We need to get in there ASAP."

"I'll transport myself there."

George half-smiled at me. "Chase tells me you have an Ancient in your back pocket. Do you think you could get her help us out with this one?"

There was a long pause before Tania replied. "Do you really think we need her? Is it that bad?"

George's face turned solemn. "Yeah, I do, Tania. I really do."

"Done. I'll be there in five." And she hung up.

George shook his head with a smile. "I think I underestimated just how much power Tania and Jaydy have both gained since the genie spell."

I took a long, steadying breath. My mate was being held captive in a house nearby, and I was just sitting there, doing nothing. My wolf reared up inside me once more. He was getting harder and harder to suppress. "Um... fuck, man. Can't we go already?"

George grabbed my arm, hard. "No! Stay right there, both of you." He hit the child lock button to lock all doors and lifted his hand. "Don't make me magick you into statues. Because I can do that."

Damon growled from the backseat, his hackles rising at being forcibly locked in like a mere mutt.

"Let us out," I demanded, growling at George through my teeth.

"Do you want to die?" George growled right back. "Because that's what's going to happen if you go charging into a witch's house. Tessie is powerful *and* crazy. And like most magicals, she is prejudiced and fucking hates shifters."

"But Jaydy—" I began.

"Jaydy is more powerful than any of us truly know," George said with a nod. "And you're no use to her dead."

"Then what's the plan?" I asked, though my body was beginning to shake. Adrenaline filled my veins as I fought the urge to shift.

"We wait for Tania to get the Ancient. Then hopefully with their magic and mine, we can lift the wards, rescue Jaydy, and take out Steve and Tessie in one fell swoop."

"And not die," I finished for him.

George nodded again with a rueful smile. "Yeah and definitely not die. Jaydy would never forgive me if I let something happen to you guys, so don't go doing anything stupid. Okay?"

"But we need to do *something*."

George's phone went off and he answered again.

"Where are you guys?" It was Tania.

George rattled off the address.

Within a moment, Tania and the Ancient who had helped our sister materialized out of thin air right in front of the truck.

"Open the doors," I repeated again.

George unlocked the doors, satisfied our back-up had arrived.

We all jumped out, ready for action.

The Ancient stared hard at Damon as he walked slowly up to her in his wolf form.

"Thank you for coming to help us again," I said to her, bowing my head respectfully, having no idea how to properly address her.

The Ancient looked at me, then my brother. "You aren't protected," she observed. "You..." She pointed to me. "Shift into your wolf, and I will give you both a gift."

I didn't bother asking Tania or even thinking twice. This woman had saved Tabby, and Jaydy trusted her.

So I will too.

I let go of my human body and shifted into my wolf to stand beside my brother.

The Ancient cast a spell over us.

A shiver coursed over my skin and a tingle of pain made my head drop, but I didn't fall, and neither did Damon. The pain persisted until it was suddenly gone, as if it had never been.

"What did you do?" Tania asked, voicing what I'd been thinking, but was unable to ask.

"It's a protection spell against magic," the Ancient answered, her voice hoarse. "I would never grant such a gift to a shifter normally, but today they're going to need it if they want to save their mate."

I bowed my head to her once more and listened to the magicals begin plotting their next steps. We were going to rescue Jaydy, and we were now armed with a magical shield of protection.

"We have a real chance," I told Damon through our unique brotherly bond,

My heart lifted with hope at the thought as adrenaline sang through my veins.

We're going to get her back, no matter what it takes!

CHAPTER 23

JAYDY

My body trembled despite my best efforts to remain calm. I didn't want them to know I was afraid, but I couldn't exert that kind of willpower over my body right now. I was just reacting and that's all there was to it.

Tessie hummed softly to herself as she lit candles around the room. Then she began smiling in a strangely serene way and turned to stare at me.

I turned my head, scrunched my lips, and looked away, unable to control the anger in my gaze. I hated them both desperately. If the hurts of the past weren't enough, today definitely took the cake and fucking iced it. They were going to kill me, *actually kill me*, and she was glad about it.

I still didn't know how I was going to do it, but I had to find a way to stop them or at least slow them down.

Maybe I can buy myself and my mates some time.

I swallowed to clear my throat and aimed for a pleading tone that would ger her attention. "Can't we come to a solution together?" I asked. "I'm sure there's a spell we can cast where I can willingly transfer my magic to you."

Tessie giggled like a maniac, like I'd just told her the funniest joke. "And why would you do that?" she scoffed.

"Because I want to *live*, and this spell is going to kill me," I fired back before softening my tone as best I could. "Look, the truth is I don't care about my magic like you do. It means nothing to me."

I liked being a witch, it was part of who I was, like my blue eyes and big ass. But I could let it go if it meant living to see another day.

No question. Just being alive with my mates is the most important thing!

"What about your job?" Tessie asked me, coming closer. "You won't be able to work at the magic school if you have no powers."

"I don't care about my job," I lied calmly. "I don't need the income, I just did it to fill in time." That was partly true. The money I'd received from my parents' inheritance would keep me fed and my house was already paid off. "Damon's a lawyer too, a successful one," I said, pushing on, feeling desperate.

Steve began to set up the table and spell books.

"He'll be happy for me to be a stay-at-home wife and not have any powers or a job." That was also partly true, and since it fed into Steve's delusions about women and their place in life, I had no problem barking out the lies if it helped save my life.

Steve's head came up from where he was focused on the spell, and he narrowed his gaze at me. "I thought you said this relationship was new?"

"It is," I defended, "but it's serious." That was the full truth.

There was a stretched, tense moment of silence as Tessie and Steve looked at one another, clearly mulling the possibility of my proposition over.

"I don't care about my magic," I repeated, "You can have it." If I'd known that the genie spell would mean the end of my life, I would have actually stopped working out and let my magic fade.

Nothing is more precious than life.

Tessie walked over to Steve, and they began whispering to each other.

I couldn't make out what they were saying, but it was obvious from their aggressive tones they weren't agreeing. I rested my head back against the table and bit back the tears that threatened to fall. I hated being tied up like this, feeling helpless and small. I'd been many things over the course of my life. Afraid, tired, embarrassed, ashamed, and alone.

But never helpless and never small.

And I hated them even more for making me feel like this at the bitter end. And what's worse, if they did it their way and I died...

My boys.

"Nope!" Tessie announced, twirling around to face me once more. "Nope... we can't do that. We can't trust you. You'll turn us into the authorities, and besides..." She reached over my face and ran her fingernails down my nose and cheek, chanting a spell in a low voice.

I tried to turn my head away from her touch, but suddenly couldn't move my neck at all.

Her touch lingered on my lower lip for a moment, then she moved her hand quickly, swiping her pointed nail against my flesh and drawing blood.

"Ow..." I complained, licking my lips and tasting the distinctly metallic tang.

Tessie the Super Bitch walked over to the spell book and lifted her hand, letting a drop of my blood fall onto the page.

The pain that struck me was unearthly. A loud gasp caught in my throat as my head was thrown back and my spine arched violently, my entire body lifting from the table beneath me. Pain was everywhere, like a million fire ants were biting me all at once. There was fire in my blood, in my veins, and in my heart. A strangled gasp caught in my throat as I tried to block out the pain.

It isn't real. It's just a spell.

I would not scream... I would not scream... I would not give them that. "Oh... God... help me."

Tessie and Steve began to chant, their spell one that I'd never heard before. One that I knew only the evilest witches and warlocks would ever conceivably perform.

No!

"Argh!" I started to scream, fighting the agony and the ropes that bound me. My magic was whirling inside me, fighting back against the spell threatening to strip my blood right from my very veins. Lightning shot from my fingertips, the carpet around me bursting into flames.

Steve waved his hand and extinguished the fire my magic had created and then continued the spell.

My belly churned painfully, and I choked back the vomit that rose up my throat, hot and sour. My skin crawled with agony. Without thinking, I cast another spell, then another, the windows in the living room shattering one after another in shimmering bursts of glass.

A white light began to glow all around me, and I fell back hard against the table as if I'd been slammed down with the blunt force of a baseball bat. My eyes closed without my permission, and a wave of tingling cold washed over me.

I'm dying.

I could feel it. My ability to fight was gone, I was too weak now. Whatever wickedness was in the spell, it had sapped me of my strength just as it was returning to me. My heart ached and my mind, still intact, rebelled.

All those years spent chasing some sort of happiness, only to lose it now.

How tragic was I? What a waste.

My poor mates... this is going to kill them.

Unable to do anything about it, I felt my soul floating away. Not even the excruciating pain could keep me inside my own body.

Damon... Chase... where are you? I need to see you, just one last time.

The room exploded in a cacophony of chaos so epic and unexpected that it caught me unaware. There were voices everywhere, their volume broken only by the sound of an ear-splitting sound.

Without warning, I was smashed back into my body, the intense pain robbing me of breath. I felt weak and pulverized, but I was alive! I forced my eyes open by sheer force of will, and a battle raged on all around me.

George was throwing magic left and right, furniture flying toward Steve and Tessie. The chairs evaporated, and George lunged for my ex, wrapping his hands around his throat.

Tessie turned toward me, her eyes blazing with malice. She was going to kill me out of spite now.

"No!"

Two huge wolves plunged into the room, both going straight for Tessie.

She turned to throw a spell at them, blasting one of them straight in the chest.

I cried out in horror as that wolf fell, my voice lost in the sounds of battle and destruction.

The second wolf made it through and bowled her over with brutal force.

I couldn't tell the guys apart yet, but my heart screamed for the wolf who was still on the floor. How badly was he hurt? Would he get up? My soul wailed at the mere notion that he may not.

"Stop!" The command echoed around us.

Everyone in the room froze, still as stone, except for me.

The Ancient walked into the room, one gnarled hand held in the air, her fingers squeezed into a tight fist.

Tania ran in behind the Ancient and made a beeline straight for me. Running her hands over my bindings, she cut them with her magic. "Jaydy. Jaydy! Are you okay?" she cried, her eyes wide and filled with emotion.

I sat up gingerly, raising my hands to my head, where my scalp still burned with pain. I threaded my fingers through my hair, and it came out in chunks. But I was alive. I was whole.

My wolves!

"Yes! Quick... please... Damon..."

Tania broke the last of the ropes tying me down.

I thew myself off the table, then fell to my knees, my legs giving out beneath me.

"Tania, hurry," the Ancient whispered, her whole body shaking with the exertion and magic required to maintain the spell. "I'm almost spent."

"Oh, yes!" Tania ran to a frozen Steve and Tessie, conjuring rope through her magic and tying them up. They weren't going anywhere, but they still had their magic.

I crawled over to my wolves, still frozen by the Ancient's magic.

"Jaydy, help me!" Tania called out, still working hard to hold my captors.

I threw my arm out and thrust every last bit of strength and magic I had left into a single spell. I cast a magic dampening net over the pair of trolls who had tried so desperately to destroy me, then fell onto the carpet, breathing hard, my heart racing.

The Ancient walked over and checked the strength of the spell binding Steve and Tessie, then dropped her arm with a groan, satisfied it would hold. "I must go." Then she was gone, just like that, disappearing back to her home, I had to assume.

That woman is incredible.

With the Ancient's spell now broken, everyone sprung back to life. The assholes who'd tried to kill me struggled against my spell net and Tania's bindings.

"Stay right there!" Tania growled at them. "The Magic Council is on the way."

My wolves began to shift back to their human forms, and it was Damon who had been hit with the spell. He wasn't moving.

Oh, God. No.

"Damon." I ran my hand through his thick dark hair, tears clogging my throat. "My love," I sobbed. "Can you hear me?"

Damon mercifully opened his eyes. With Tessie's magic bound, he was able to sit up, and he reached out to me. "Yeah, I'm okay. Are you?"

I threw myself into his arms, feeling the heat of his naked body against my face. It was like heaven. "I was *so* scared. I thought I was going to lose you both."

Chase knelt down and cupped my face tenderly. "We're so glad you're safe. We're not going anywhere."

"You guys should get out of here," George said, puffing like he'd run a marathon.

"But what about Jaydy?" Chase argued, standing up to talk to George directly.

"She has to stay and tell the Magic Council what Steve and Tessie did."

I sat up, wiping away the tears from my cheeks. "Yes," I agreed. "I need to stay."

Damon got to his feet also, naked and beautiful. "We want to stay with you."

Together, they helped me to my feet.

I grabbed their hands, squeezing them tightly. "The Council doesn't like shifters, and I want to make sure Steve and Tessie get thrown in jail. Please, go. I'll be okay now."

Chase kissed me, clearly not wanting to leave me.

Then Damon did the same. Pulling me into his arms, he pressed his lips against mine in a desperate bid for connection.

I knew just how he felt because I was feeling the exact same thing.

"We'll see you at home?" Chase asked, his gaze locked on me.

I smiled as I realized he meant their house.

Our house.

I nodded with relief. "Yes. I'll come over as soon as we're done here."

The guys nodded. They would go, but they didn't like it.

George threw his keys to Damon. "Here, take my truck. I'll come by later and pick it up."

"Thanks, bud," Damon said as he reached out and shook George's hand.

I stared at Damon, still rattled from seeing him go down during the fray. "Are you sure you're okay?" I asked, again, running my hands over his muscled arms. "I was so terrified when Tessie hit you with that spell."

Damon grinned at me. "Thanks to your Ancient friend, Chase and I have new magical armor."

I frowned at him in confusion. "What do you mean?"

George waved them off. "I'll explain," he promised. "You guys go. The Council is moments away."

The guys stole one more kiss each before they ran out of the house.

I had one minute to breathe before the Council arrived to assess the situation and take control of the mess at hand. That's when I got the whole story from George and Tania. I couldn't help but cry through the interviews, knowing my friends and my mates loved me so much made my heart ache with joy and gratitude.

I'd fought for my life today, and it was a life that I could finally say was entirely worth fighting for.

CHAPTER 24

CHASE

As soon as we got back to our huge house, I started cooking. I needed to do *something* useful while we waited for Jaydy to come home.

Meanwhile, Damon wore a path in the carpet from pacing so hard. "She's on her way!" Damon called out. "She just sent a text."

I put my hands on the kitchen counter, dropped my head, and closed my eyes. "Thank God." Part of me had been afraid that their Magic Council might hold her all night or charge her with something ludicrous. I'd seen more than my fair share of innocent people arrested in my time as a lawyer.

Damon walked into the kitchen a moment later and sniffed the air. "Smells good," he said.

"Yeah, meatloaf, mashed potatoes, gravy, and apple pie." Normal comfort food. Things I knew Jaydy would really appreciate. It had been over three hours since we'd arrived home, and I was dying to have our mate back in our arms. A timely knock on the front door had us both running toward the foyer. "It's open!" I called out, and the door opened just as we reached it.

"Hey, guys!" Jaydy gushed as she walked in with Meg cuddled in her arms.

We rushed her, hugging her tightly.

Meg mewled in protest, so we leaned back to accommodate her.

"Come," I said, tugging her toward the living room. "We have a place for Meg now too." I gestured to the newly decorated "cat corner" of our spacious living room. It was now fitted out with a huge cat scratching house, climbing frame, and a plush, new, cozy bed.

"Oh, guys, this is so thoughtful!" Jaydy gushed. "What do you think, Meg?"

The cat jumped down from her arms and sauntered over to the corner of the room, circling her bed twice before lying down amongst the comfortable pillows with an exaggerated yawn.

I laughed as I tugged our mate back into my arms and held her once more.

Damon put his arms around her also and we stood there, just breathing in her scent for a long time.

Eventually, Jaydy lifted her head with a meek smile of apology. "I have to sit down."

"This way," I said, taking her hand. "I cooked lunch or dinner or whatever meal this is." I didn't know what time it was, and I didn't care. I just wanted to look after her and cater to her every desire.

Jaydy smiled at me, tears in her beautiful blue eyes. "Thank you. I'm starving."

We took her to the kitchen and got her to sit on a barstool at the counter. "You can have everything or nothing. We'll order in if this isn't what you feel like." I started to serve the food even though I wasn't sure if she wanted me to or not.

"Oh, I'll have *everything*, thank you. It looks amazing."

We all sat down to eat around the counter.

I managed to get some of the meat and potatoes down, but my stomach was twisted up in knots. "Can you tell us what happened?" I asked gently, not wanting to upset or exhaust her further if she didn't feel like talking.

She recalled the scene with greater excitement than I'd expected. The Council had heard Jaydy's testimony, then Tania and George's. Then they'd put a truth spell on Steve and Tessie, and it had spilled out of them.

"Is that even legal?" I asked, wishing we had that sort of tool available in our system. A spell that could make anyone tell the truth would be a brilliant tool for a lawyer on the right side of the law.

She shrugged as she spooned more apple pie in her mouth, sighing with blissful contentment. "The Council wasn't taking any chances on this one," she explained.

"So, what'll happen to them?" I asked, "I'm hoping they'll be thrown into a locked hole, and the key thrown away."

"Basically, that's exactly what's going to happen to them," she said, pouring an extra helping of luxurious ice cream on the pie. "I can't believe I missed the comp, though."

Damon burst out laughing. "Only *you* would say that after a day like today."

She shrugged. "I'm getting back to feeling like myself, I guess."

I glanced at my brother, then back to my mate.

Our mate.

"Jaydy, when you were taken..."

"I know." She smiled. "You were worried."

"We were devastated," I corrected. "We couldn't even imagine losing you. I..."

Damon took her hand, saying what I apparently couldn't. "Jaydy, we want you to mate with us. We want you to marry us, as soon as possible."

Jaydy put her fork down, her lips falling open in surprise. "You want to... you mean, like Tania's wedding?"

"We can do it any way you like," I said, finding my words once more with a wave of my hand. "It can be a big, extravagant event, anywhere you want. Or it can be small and intimate. It doesn't matter to us, beautiful. We just want *you*."

"But what's the rush?" she asked, looking between us, her eyes big, wide. Scared. "Is this because of today? I don't want you making decisions from a place of fear."

I smiled as reassuringly as I could. "Oh, sweetheart, we're not rushing. We've been waiting for you our *entire* lives."

"But..."

Damon squeezed her arm, lending her his strength. "No buts. We want you, Jaydy. And we want you to know that we're yours, and you're ours. There's no question for us."

Asking her to marry us now was a gamble. She'd freaked out the first time we'd talked about the concept of forever, but I couldn't stop the words from pouring out of me, and Damon seemed to feel exactly the same way.

She gulped, her blue eyes filling with tears. "There's no question for me either."

The breath I'd been holding whooshed out of my lungs, and I nearly levitated off my barstool. "So that's a yes?" I asked, quickly walking around the counter.

She nodded with a sheepish grin.

I pulled her to her feet and spun her around. "Now, we need to take you shopping for a ring!"

She grinned at me.

I cupped her face, pressing my forehead against hers and closing my eyes. We had her back with us, and she was safe. I still couldn't believe it.

"But first..." Damon began.

I opened my eyes and turned toward him.

He smiled broadly. "Let's take you to bed and celebrate being alive."

Now that would be the best way to reassure myself that she was really okay.

"Oh, yes, please!" Jaydy squealed, giggling as she ran ahead of us.

We practically chased her to the master bedroom.

There was desperation in the air now, I could smell it.

She began to strip, pulling at her clothes, not slowing down until she was completely naked.

Damon and I followed her lead.

"Damn, you're beautiful," I said, staring at her beautiful curves and luscious, milky flesh. I dropped the last of my clothes and surged toward her. Putting my hands around her waist and pulling her naked, warm body against mine, I kissed her lips, hard, sliding my tongue into her mouth and tasting her sweetness.

Damon joined us, stepping in behind her and began cupping her breasts and kissing a trail down her neck.

I pulled back and panted. "Get on the bed. I want to taste you."

Jaydy walked over to the bed without hesitation, swinging her hips with confidence in a seductive way that made me want to just push her down on the mattress and fuck us both into oblivion.

Damn, she is sexy.

Jaydy lay down and opened her thighs for me, inviting me to fulfil my own desires.

I licked my lips, suddenly ravenous, and pushed her legs further apart, kneeling down to lick her pussy.

Damon got onto the bed and kissed Jaydy's lips before working his way down her body to suckle at her breasts, tweaking and teasing them with his teeth.

We worked on her until she was crying out for us to stop.

I lifted my head. "What do you need now, beautiful?"

"Both of you," she panted, getting up and arranging herself on the corner of the bed, on her hands and knees. "*Please.*"

I moved in behind her, not willing to wait a moment longer. I slid my hands over her perfect hips and ass. "Damn, you look fucking amazing like this. And if you don't believe me..." I came forward, using my erect cock to paint my wetness along her pink flesh.

"Oh, please," she moaned. "Please. Yes."

"You're going to marry us, right, sweetheart?"

"Oh, yes," she whispered.

Damon stepped in front of her, offering himself to her lush lips.

She moved forward and took his cock into her mouth.

Damon threw his head back, moaning loudly.

I savored the moment, just watching her bountiful ass bounce with her every movement, before spearing her pussy with my cock. Her hot wetness engulfed me, sending thrills of ecstasy to my core.

Jaydy gasped and pressed back against me, eager for more. Then our dance of passion and raw need truly began. The three of us moved as one—one family—one mate and her shifter men.

I fucked Jaydy long and hard, relishing in every moan and gasp. Every time her pussy squeezed my cock, I was glad to be alive. This was what life was about. The love and connection we shared between us. It was everything.

Sweat rolled down my back as I moved deep inside her. Soon, she'd have our baby. Soon, she'd be our wife, and our lives would be perfect.

Damon came first, calling out to the heavens as his orgasm hit him like a freight train, setting off a chain reaction.

Jaydy's back arched beneath my hands and her pussy clamped down on my cock, *hard*. Her orgasm called to mine with its siren song.

I didn't hold back, unable to even if I tried. I thrust deep inside my perfect, beautiful mate and filled her sweet pussy with my seed.

When the waves of our rapture were utterly spent, we finally all collapsed in a pile of limbs and satisfied sighs.

This is bliss. Pure bliss.

I reached over and kissed Jaydy on the lips, my heart full. "I love you, beautiful girl."

She teared up, her smile wobbly. "I love you too," she whispered. Then she turned to Damon and repeated her promise.

Exhausted, I closed my eyes, happy in the knowledge that we were finally, the three of us, complete.

EPILOGUE

JAYDY

Two weeks later.

Damon led me inside his parents' house, and we sat down on the sofas, just as we had, all those weeks ago. But this time, we weren't here to talk about Tabby, we were here to announce our engagement.

The stunning diamond ring the boys had bought me lay heavy and warm on my finger. I couldn't believe how big and beautiful it was.

Just like me...

My mates had truly spoiled me, and the sparkler took my breath away every single time I took a moment to admire it.

"Hey, Mom, Dad! We're here."

Nancy came down the hallway with a big smile on her face. "Jaydy! Boys! It's so good to see you," she said as she pulled me into her arms and hugged me.

I froze with shock for a moment before melting into her arms. "Hi, Nancy."

She led us into the large dining room, which had been set up for dinner with a pretty tablecloth, candles, and crockery. "I hope you're hungry," she said. "I've got all the boys' favorites, which pretty much means we've got every type of meat under the sun in one form or another!"

"I'm always hungry," I managed to say, even though my throat was thick with nerves and emotion.

Nancy laughed. "It must be all that training you do. Chase was telling me the other day about Tania's gym and your competitions. It's such a pity you missed the last one."

A strangled laugh burst out of my throat, and I smiled awkwardly, unsure of how much the boys had shared with their parents about what went down that day. "Oh... yeah. That wasn't a good day. But Tania's hosting the next one in three months, so I'll be there."

"Well, that's wonderful, Jaydy. I can't wait to cheer you on. But for now, come, sit," Nancy said, indicating to the table with a sweeping gesture.

The guys chivalrously held out a chair for me, then sat on either side of me, flanking me like my very own personal bodyguards.

"Where's Dad?" Damon asked.

"In the shower," Nancy said. "Tabby and your dad have been out all day. Ever since Tabby got her legs back, she wants to shift and run, *all* the time." Nancy blinked back tears as she smiled. "We just don't have the heart to say no, not after all that she's been through. All the time's she lost."

Chase put an arm around the back of my chair. "That's great, Mom. Maybe we should come by and run with Tabby on weekends? It'd take some of the stress off Dad."

"Oh, you're always welcome to," Nancy said, handing Chase a bottle of red wine and a corkscrew.

He obediently stood up to open it, following his mother's non-verbal instructions.

"But it's good exercise for your dad now that he's retired," she added.

"And I'll never say no to a run with my sons." Bill's booming voice sounded in the room as he walked in, tall as a tree.

My heart always ached when I saw the man who'd fathered my mates. He'd carried so much sorrow and pain for so long. But today, he looked ten years younger. "Hi, Jaydy," he said with a nod.

"Hi, Bill," I said, and couldn't help adding, "You look so well."

Nancy sidled up next to him, putting a hand on his chest. "Doesn't he?"

We all murmured our agreement, and it was nice to be in such a relaxed, family atmosphere.

Tabby bounced in the room, looking fit and happy. "Jaydy!" she cried.

I rose to my feet to hug my mates' baby sister. "Hey, Tabby! It's *so* good to see you. I hear you've been giving your dad the run around!" I pulled back gently.

"I really have!" She laughed, then scarcely a heartbeat later, Tabby's eyes went wide before she grabbed my hand and held it firmly. "Oh my God. Is that..."

"Oh... ah..." I pulled away.

Damn it! I've ruined the surprise.

"Yeah. I didn't want to take it off." I'd been worried one of the eagle-eyed wolves would see my ring before the announcement, but it was way too expensive for me to take off and leave anywhere. Not only that, but I was attached. What it represented meant a great deal to me.

Tabby began to squeal with excitement.

My mates came up around me, their arms around my waist, stopping me from backing away any further.

"Tabby, hold it together for one minute," Damon told his sister.

She managed to close her mouth, but her eyes were big and wild.

Chase shook his head and sighed. "Mom, Dad, we came to dinner to tell you that we asked Jaydy to mate with us, and she's accepted."

"Oh my God! Yes! I get a sister! Finally!" Tabby yelled, bouncing straight at me.

If the guys hadn't been holding me firmly, she would have knocked me flat on my back with her enthusiasm. "So do I," I whispered, tears filling my eyes as I pulled back and wiped my face. "Thank you, Tabby."

"For what?" She beamed, her brow briefly creasing.

"For being happy about this," I said, still feeling awkward, being the only witch in a family of wolf shifters.

"Why wouldn't I be?" she asked.

Before I could answer, Nancy came forward to hug me too. "I'm so happy," she whispered, kissing my cheek. "My boys are very lucky to have found you."

That got me right in the feels, I had to admit. And had to fight the need to sob. When I finally got myself together and pulled away, my mate's father approached.

It was Bill's turn to open his arms to me. "Welcome to the family, Jaydy."

I glanced up at Chase, who smiled at me. "Go on."

I walked into the bear hug, heavy with emotion.

Bill wrapped his arms around me, holding me tight.

I began to cry. I couldn't stop myself. I'd lost my father more than a decade ago and had missed the feeling of a dad's hug. It was warm and comforting and protective in a way only a father could be. I'd missed it so much.

"Are you okay?" Nancy asked, patting me on the back softly.

I pulled away and used my magic to clean up my face, not wanting to ruin the moment. I managed to nod and returned to the safety of Damon and Chase's arms.

"Why are you crying?" Tabby asked, the fearless girl voicing the question I was sure everyone else wanted to know.

"I just..." I indicated to her parents. "It's the whole family thing."

Chase squeezed my arm with an understanding smile. "Jaydy's parents died when she was in high school, so I think the big family thing is a good thing. Yeah, beautiful?"

I nodded. "Of course. I love my brother, but he's away at college. And I've missed having a real family."

Nancy and Bill opened their arms, moved by my words.

I stepped into their embrace without a second thought. It felt entirely natural.

Tabby jumped on us, joining the bear hug.

My mates wrapped their arms around us all, turning it into one big group hug of love and support.

My heart cracked wide open, and I immediately burst into a new wave of tears. This time, I didn't try to stop them. I'd finally found my place in this world as well as a love I thought could only possibly exist in dreams. With my mates and my new family by side, there was *nothing* that would stop me from living my best life from now on!

EPILOGUE

DANIELLA

Part Two

I reached into my large black Mary Poppins' style bag, found what I'd been looking for, and handed the bride a barley sugar candy. "My sister swears by these for morning sickness. Just suck on it."

Jaydy took the candy with a grateful smile and unwrapped the crinkly clear cellophane. "Thanks, hon. I knew when I went off birth control there was a chance, I'd fall pregnant, but I never imagined it would happen so fast!"

Tania handed Jaydy her bridal bouquet with a chuckle. "Well, my mom says morning sickness is the sign of a healthy pregnancy."

I turned to my other recently married friend. "Do you have something to tell us, Tania?"

Tania cackled with laughter. "No, not yet... not that the boys aren't trying of course!" She waggled her eyebrows at me suggestively, her lips stretched wide by her trademark grin.

I laughed but the sound rang hollow in my chest. I knew exactly what she was hinting at, and I was jealous as all hell.

Two sexy wolf shifters to love forever? Yes please!

"Feeling better?" I asked with a hopeful smile, turning my attention back to the bride.

Jaydy sucked on the candy I'd given her and paused a moment as if contemplating precisely how she felt. "Yes, actually. I feel heaps better, thank you."

"Let's do it, then!" I squeezed Jaydy's hand encouragingly and walked her to the door of the master bedroom suite.

Jaydy and her men were getting married at Bill and Nancy's property. Leo and Mason had offered to build a deck and pergola for them as a wedding gift, but between Jaydy, Tania and I, we'd conjured up an incredible event. With no neighbors in sight, there wasn't anyone to complain or suspect anything out of the ordinary when new landscaping and buildings suddenly appeared overnight.

The bedroom door opened, and Jaydy's baby brother bounced into the room with a swish and a bow. "I'm here!" he announced.

"Late as always," I said to Nicky, kissing his cheek. "You're looking good, kiddo."

Nicky grinned at me, then offered his arm to his big sister. "Ready, Sis?"

She inhaled deeply, resting a nervous hand on her still unswollen belly. "Yes. Definitely."

Together we walked through the doors and out into the magically manicured back gardens. I led the procession, following the white rose petal strewn walkway, proudly wearing my new royal purple bridesmaid dress. Tania and Jaydy sashayed close behind me.

Jaydy had chosen a gorgeous black and white theme embellished with purple and gold. The accents were noticeable throughout the striking flower arrangements, the men's ties, and the general festive décor of the venue. The dresses she'd chosen for us were the perfect style for us larger-than-life girls, and I was proud as punch to stand up with my friend on her most special of days.

I arrived at the floral archway first and beamed at Jaydy's two handsome grooms. They were like night and day in their appearance, but wore twin looks of love on their faces as they stared in awe at their bride.

The ceremony ended up being a lovely combination of wolf shifter mating ceremony oaths as well as the necessary legal jargon required by the State for the marriage to be recognized. It was beautiful, heartfelt, and just... *perfect*. When the ceremony concluded, Jaydy and her men were whisked away for photos and not long after, Tania went missing with her men too.

I didn't need to wonder where they'd gone or why. I knew they wouldn't be able to go long without laying claim to her again after we'd all shared in such a beautiful ceremony. So, I sat by myself at the bridal table, grateful to be a part of the crew. I'd trained at Tania's gym for so many years she'd hired me for reception last year and I now worked there full time. And Jaydy... well, Jaydy was like a sister to me. We were all really close—our very own found family.

"Um... hello. You must be Daniella." The words, spoken by a deep and unfamiliar voice, broke me out of my reverie.

I looked up to find a truly beautiful man. He was at least ten years older than me and had an immediate and very tangible effect on my love-starved body. I swallowed hard. "Oh, yes. Hi. That's me. But everyone just calls me Dani." I rose to my feet, smoothing my dress to speak with him properly.

His gaze ran over my body in an appreciative way, and he cleared his throat with a lop-sided smile.

"And you are...?" I asked, giggling and pursing my lips knowingly when his gaze failed to meet mine.

My eyes are up here, hon.

The handsome older man seemed to be struggling to speak but finally managed to pull himself together with some grace. "Yes! Right. Sorry. I'm Travis," he said. "I'm Bill's cousin."

I grinned at him, flattered by his fluster while noting the fine lines around his eyes and graying hair at his temples. Now that I was closer, I reassessed his age. I was thirty-two, and he was probably twenty years older than me. but

Damn he is gorgeous!

He was the literal definition of a silver fox. "Well, it's nice to meet you, Travis." I lifted my glass of wine to my lips and took a sip, cocking my brow playfully. "It was a beautiful wedding, wasn't it?"

He smiled and licked his lips, before clearing his throat again.

My belly fluttered instantly with arousal, and I unconsciously squeezed my thighs together tightly. This handsome stranger was having a serious effect on me; there was no denying it. I'd never felt anything like it.

"Yes, it was indeed."

I glanced down at his hands, but he had them firmly in his trouser pockets. He wore a rather dashing black suit and looked every bit a gentleman. "And are you married too, Travis?" I enquired, secretly hoping he was not.

"Too?" he repeated, sounding shocked as his eyes widened.

I frowned at him, momentarily thrown by his reaction. "Yeah..." I said, referring to my friend's marriage.

"Are you married?" he demanded as if caught off guard.

I laughed, more in a shocked reflex than anything else as I fiddled with my hair. "No, no. I just meant..."

Another man came rushing over and grabbed Travis by the sleeve. "We have to go. *Now*," he emphasized, glancing briefly my way.

"No," Travis said, shrugging the guy's hand off. "I told you, I'm not leaving."

"Travis..." the other guy growled, the sound sending a shiver up my spine.

Travis ignored him and turned toward me again with a decidedly exasperated smile. "Dani," he said formally, "this is my brother, Shaun."

Shaun looked to be a few years younger than Travis, but he seemed harder somehow, less refined. He was bigger in size and build, and his face was cold and more angular. He also wasn't wearing a full suit, instead opting for gray pants, a vest, and a white shirt, the sleeves rolled up to his elbows to reveal muscular forearms.

I smiled at the interloper politely and set my wine glass back on the table. "Hey. It's nice to meet you." I reached out to shake his hand in welcome, but he seemed genuinely distressed, prompting me to ask, "Are you okay?"

"No. No!" Shaun stepped back, tripping over a dip in the grass before hitting the deck in his formal attire.

"Oh, no..." I rushed around the bridal table and reached for him, grabbing his arm and helping him to his feet. "Are you okay?" I asked again, concerned and confused.

What the hell is going on with this guy?

A moment later my hand brushed his and my skin tingled like I'd just brushed fire. I pulled back, startled by the unexpected sensation. "What on Earth was that?" I gasped.

Shaun glared at his brother in response, then stormed off without so much as a backward glance.

Travis sighed, took my hand, and lifted it to his lips. His skin tingled against mine as well. The dancing flames of our connection delicious in a way that made me want to melt right into his arms. "Until next time, beautiful Daniella." He kissed my knuckles, then, like the gentleman he appeared to be, took his leave.

Breathless, my heart racing, I watched them both go. I blinked several times, trying to ground myself in reality. "Whew... that was intense." I adjusted my dress, walked back to my seat at the bridal table, and lifted my glass to my lips. I drank the rest of my sweet, crisp wine in a few quick swallows, my hand still tingling. Whatever that was... I *wanted* more.